A Mission of Mercy

Perhaps I dozed. Yes, I'm almost sure I did, because the next thing I knew, I had a foot in my face (Little Alfred's) and the tent was as dark as the inside of a crow. I sat up, yawned, blinked my eyes, and glanced around. And suddenly I realized that I had been dreaming about...bones.

Actually, that was nothing unusual. I often had bone dreams and they were always fun. Sometimes I saw myself chewing on steak bones, other times ham bones, and every once in a while, chicken bones. But this dream was different because it involved . . . well, an ancient buffalo bone. No kidding. I mean, in my dream I saw it lying in the middle of a square-shaped trench, and I was almost sure that...

I'd better not say any more because it might sound strange. I mean, bones don't talk, right? Yet this bone seemed to be calling out to me. Oops, I said it. Okay, in my dream, this bone was calling my name and asking . . . the bone was *pleading* for me to come and save it from "bondage."

The Case of the
Most Ancient Bone

by John R. Erickson

Illustrations by Gerald L. Holmes

PUFFIN BOOKS

PUFFIN BOOKS
Published by the Penguin Group
Penguin Young Readers Group, 345 Hudson Street, New York, New York 10014, U.S.A.
Penguin Group (Canada), 90 Eglinton Avenue East, Suite 700,
Toronto, Ontario, Canada M4P 2Y3 (a division of Pearson Penguin Canada Inc.)
Penguin Books Ltd, 80 Strand, London WC2R 0RL, England
Penguin Ireland, 25 St Stephen's Green, Dublin 2, Ireland
(a division of Penguin Books Ltd)
Penguin Group (Australia), 250 Camberwell Road, Camberwell, Victoria 3124, Australia
(a division of Pearson Australia Group Pty Ltd)
Penguin Books India Pvt Ltd, 11 Community Centre,
Panchsheel Park, New Delhi - 110 017, India
Penguin Group (NZ), 67 Apollo Drive, Rosedale, North Shore 0745, Auckland, New Zealand
(a division of Pearson New Zealand Ltd)
Penguin Books (South Africa) (Pty) Ltd, 24 Sturdee Avenue,
Rosebank, Johannesburg 2196, South Africa

Registered Offices: Penguin Books Ltd, 80 Strand, London WC2R 0RL, England

Published simultaneously in the United States of America by Viking Children's Books
and Puffin Books, divisions of Penguin Young Readers Group, 2007

1 3 5 7 9 10 8 6 4 2

LIBRARY OF CONGRESS CATALOGING-IN-PUBLICATION DATA

Erickson, John R., date–
The case of the most ancient bone / by John R. Erickson ;
illustrations by Gerald L. Holmes.
p. cm. — (Hank the Cowdog ; 50)
Summary: When Hank the Cowdog, Head of Ranch Security, follows Little Alfred to an
archaeological excavation, he runs into trouble in the form of a gorgeous golden-haired
lady dog, a peanut butter sandwich, and an enticing, ancient, buffalo bone.
ISBN 978-0-14-240800-1 (pbk.) — ISBN 978-0-670-06224-9 (hardcover)
[1. Archaeology—Fiction. 2. Bones—Fiction. 3. Dogs—Fiction.
4. Ranch life—West (U.S.)—Fiction. 5. West (U.S.)—Fiction. 6. Humorous stories.
7. Mystery and detective stories.] I. Holmes, Gerald L., ill II. Title.
PZ7.E72556Camo 2007   [Fic]—dc22   2006031057

Puffin Books ISBN 978-0-14-240800-1

*#50 has to be dedicated to the gal
who brung me to the dance,
Kris Erickson, my wife of 39 years.
With love and gratitude.*

CONTENTS

CHAPTER ONE

Unbearable Heat!

It's me again, Hank the Cowdog. The drama began around the end of July, a very hot and ugly part of the year. It wasn't a great time for me to fall madly in love with Sardina Bandana or to launch myself into a new career, but things always have a way of happening when they happen.

We'd had week after week of awful heat and no rain. All the ponds on the ranch dried up, and the creek turned into a ribbon of sand. Why, it was so dry that wild animals were coming up to headquarters to drink water from the stock tanks in the corrals, and we're talking about roadrunners, deer, skunks, raccoons, and even coyotes.

Yes sir, coyotes. In normal times, a coyote

1

won't go anywhere near a place where people stay, but the combination of heat and thirst had made them even bolder and more dangerous than normal. As you will see, that will cause serious problems later in the story, but that's later in the story and we're not there yet, so forget I mentioned it.

We were discussing heat. There are certain times when a dog has energy and ambition, and there are times when he just . . . melts, tries to hide from the hateful glare of the sun, and wishes that the summer would come to an end already.

That's the way it was that day in July. Ugly weather. It was the middle of the morning and already the air was hot and still. Heat waves shimmered on the horizon. The pastures were parched and brown, the grass so brittle that it crackled under your feet. The trees were wilted. Even the weeds were wilted. The roads were so dry they had turned to powder. When a vehicle approached, you could see it coming for miles, throwing up a long plume of dust.

Drover and I had done our routine patrols in the cool of morning. Then, at nine o'clock, we shifted into our Dog Maintenance Program. Are you familiar with the DMP? Maybe not, so let's go over it. Pay attention. I don't want to have to repeat myself. It's too hot.

The Dog Maintenance Program is our way of conserving our precious reserves of energy and coping with terrible heat. The first thing we do is find a nice piece of shade. Next, we scratch up the ground and remove the top layer of soil. Why? Simple. In the middle of summer, the ground is hot. To find a cooler layer of dirt, we have to do some digging, which is too bad, because digging just makes us even hotter.

But once we remove the top two inches of soil, we have ourselves a little hole into which we can pour our molten bodies. We flop down into our holes and proceed to the Second Phase of the DMP, in which we . . . well, we don't do much of anything, to be honest, and that's the whole point of the DMP. We pant for air and let drops of water drip off our respective tongues. When the need arises, we flick our ears to ward off pesky flies and hateful wasps.

But mostly what we do in the DMP is . . . *stare*. We stare out at the heat waves shimmering on the horizon. We stare at the dust clouds created by vehicles on the county road. We stare at the wild turkeys huddled under the shade of nearby

trees. We pant and stare at the turkeys, and they pant and stare back at us.

Does that sound pretty boring? It is, but that's what we do in the heat of summer. We pant and stare and . . . I don't know, wait for winter to come, I suppose.

That's what we were doing on that particular morning. Drover and I had initiated the Dog Maintenance Program and were waiting for a blizzard to rescue us from the heat, when all at once I noticed . . .

"Drover, why are you staring at me?"

He blinked his eyes and grinned. "Oh, hi. Did you say something?"

"I did, yes. I asked why you're staring at me."

"Oh. Was I staring at you?"

"Yes. That's why I asked the question. What's the answer?"

"Well, let me think here. What was the question again?"

"Why are you staring at me?"

"Oh. You noticed?"

"Of course I noticed. Answer the question and hurry up."

"Well, I guess I was staring at you because . . . I didn't have the energy to stare at anything else. It's hot out here."

"I realize that it's hot, Drover, but how much energy would it take for you to move your eyeballs one inch to the left or right? That's all it would take, you see. Just move your eyeballs one inch."

"Which way?"

"I don't care. Just move them." He moved his gaze one inch to the left. "Thanks. I know that was asking a lot, but I appreciate it."

There was a moment of silence. "How come I can't stare at you?"

"Because I don't enjoy being stared at."

"Well . . ." A quiver came into his voice. "It kind of hurts my feelings."

"Oh brother. Look, what if I sat around all day, staring at you? How would you like that?"

"I wouldn't care. That's what friends are for."

"Okay, buddy, we'll put that to the test. I will now direct my gaze at you and *stare*, and we'll just see how you like it."

I went to the huge effort of shifting my eyeballs two full inches to the left and began the Staring Procedure. Oh, and I even narrowed my eyes, just to put a little edge on my gaze. Minutes passed and soon I began to feel the strain.

"What do you say now? How does it feel to be stared at, huh?"

"It doesn't bother me."

"Of course it bothers you. Nobody enjoys being stared at. Why don't you just come out and admit it?"

"'Cause I don't care. I'm too hot to care."

"Okay, fine. I'll keep it up. I'll stare at you for the rest of the day."

I continued to direct my gaze toward Drover's face and let my eyes blur into his murfing mork ponking honkeypoof . . . let my eyes bore into his . . . snerk muff mork . . .

The heat, the terrible heat was burning me up and all at once I was having trouble . . . snorff . . . keeping my pielids . . . keeping my eyelids open, shall we say, and I felt my inner self being pulled into the dark tunnel of . . . zzzzzzzzzzzzzzzz.

Suddenly I heard a voice from outside the tunnel. It said, and this is a direct quote, it said, "How come you quit staring at me?"

My eyelids quivered, and I heard myself say, "It wasn't me, you can't prove a thing." Then . . . hmmm . . . my vision returned to the present moment and I found myself looking into the eyes of . . . Drover. "Oh, it's you again. What were we discussing? I seem to have lost the thread of my train . . . the train of my track . . . my train of thought."

He grinned. "Well, you said you were going to stare at me all day, but I think you fell asleep."

"Yes, of course, it's all coming back to me now." I pushed myself up on all-fours and shook the vapors out of my head. "Drover, this heat is destroying our lives. It's forcing us into irrational forms of behavior, such as staring at each other. It's even leading us into loony conversations. If we don't do something to fight against the forces of chaos, we'll sink into the mire and become a couple of worthless dogs."

He yawned. "Gosh, what should we do?"

I began pacing, as I often do when my mind has shifted into a higher level. "We'll fight back, Drover. We'll get up off our duffs and call upon our reserves of Iron Discipline. We're cowdogs, don't ever forget that."

"Not me. I'm just a mutt."

"Okay, you're just a mutt, but I'm a cowdog, and cowdogs have always been just a little bit special. Here's the plan. On the count of three, we will . . ." Suddenly my legs wilted and I collapsed to the ground. "On the count of three, we will do nothing."

"I think I can handle that."

"Because this heat is killing us."

"Yeah, it's hot."

"And the terrible heat has melted our reserves of Iron Discipline and turned us into chicken soup."

"Boy, I love soup."

"But that doesn't mean that you can stare at me, Drover. It's an invasion of my privacy and I will not tolerate it, do you understand?"

He yawned again. "What?"

"I said, this private invasion of my tolerance must stop!"

"I thought it was chicken soup."

"Of course it was chicken soup, but that doesn't mean you can't be intolerant once in a while."

He gave me a blank stare. "I think I missed something."

I gave him a blank stare. "Yes, I'm getting that same feeling myself. It's the heat, Drover. It's causing us to babble and behave like lunatics."

"Oh no. What should we do?"

I cut my eyes from side to side. It was a moment of decision. "Let's . . . let's just lie here and do nothing. We'll wait for the first snowstorm of the season."

"Yeah, and maybe we should stare at each other."

9

"Great idea. Okay, now we have a plan. On the count of three, we'll put our plan into action."

"Someone's coming."

"I beg your pardon?"

Drover pointed a paw toward a cloud of dust to the north. "Someone's coming. I think it's a pickup."

"You know what? I don't care."

"Yeah, me neither." After a few moments, he said, "I bet that pickup's coming to the machine shed, right where we are."

"I still don't care."

"Yeah, but we're right in the way. What if he runs over us?"

I ran that report through Data Control. "Maybe we should move."

I hated to go to so much trouble, but it's a good thing we did. Moments later, an unidentified pickup rolled up in front of the machine shed doors. If we hadn't moved, we might have gotten smashed flat as two pancakes.

Windmill Problems

Perhaps you're asking yourself, "If it was an unidentified pickup, why didn't the dogs bark at it?" Great question. As you know, barking at strangers is an important part of our job on this outfit, and very seldom do we miss an opportunity to do it.

This time, we did. Why? Too hot. But it would have been a waste of time anyway, because it turned out that it wasn't an unidentified pickup after all. The pickup belonged to our ranch. Slim and Loper had come back to the machine shed for some supplies or equipment.

When they stepped out of the pickup, my keen eyes picked up an important clue: Loper was having a bad day. He looked mad and disgusted.

The moment his boots touched the ground, he growled, "The stinking windmill pumped all winter and never missed a stroke. When we didn't need the water, it gave us water, water, and more water. Now it's hot and what does it do? It quits pumping and we've got fifty cows, standing on their heads at the tank, trying to get a drink!"

Slim nodded and shifted his toothpick to the left side of his mouth. "It don't seem fair, does it?"

"No! It makes me so mad . . ."

Slim waited to hear the rest of the sentence. When it didn't come, he said, "But you know what? I think a hurricane might be worse."

Loper turned halfway around and stared at him for a long moment. "What?"

"If we ranched down on the Gulf coast, we'd have hurricanes and then we'd have to worry about floods. Your cows might be swimming around and hung up in the tops of trees. You wouldn't like that either."

Loper turned his gaze to the ground and shook his head. "Slim, that is the dumbest thing you've said in two weeks."

"No, it ain't. All I'm saying is that a man shouldn't complain about his problems, 'cause there might be worse problems in this old world."

"Slim, this is *my* ranch and if I want to complain about a busted windmill in the middle of a heatwave, I'll complain about it."

"I know you will, 'cause that's all you've been doing for the past thirty minutes."

"The Constitution of the United States of America gives me the right to complain about ignorant windmills."

"Loper, every now and then, a man ought to stop whining and count his blessings."

Loper gave him a ferocious glare. "Whining, huh? All right, buddy, I'll count my blessings: one, two, three. There, are you happy?"

"No, you didn't say what they are."

Loper began slashing a finger through the air. "Blessing Number One is that you're not twins. Blessing Number Two is that at the end of a long hot day, I don't have to eat your bachelor cooking. Blessing Number Three is that I've got a radio in that pickup, so when you start yapping about blessings, I can turn up the volume. There!"

"Loper, you're worse than a mule. You didn't say a word about being grateful that we don't have floods and earthquakes and bluebonnet plague."

"Yeah? Well, I'm not. I'm mad at the windmill and I plan to stay mad until we get it fixed . . . speaking of which, do you suppose you could start gathering up our windmill tools?"

Slim shifted his toothpick over to the other side of his mouth. "Well, I probably could, but I still say . . ."

"Good!" Loper whirled around and headed for the machine shed. "We'll need the block and tackle, a box of windmill leathers, a chain, wrenches, a socket set . . ." He vanished inside the barn, and his voice became a faint rumble.

Slim heaved a sigh and looked down at me. "His momma enrolled him in charm school, but he flunked out. Pooch, you want to go in my place and help Uncle Scrooge fix the windmill?"

Uh . . . no thanks. I had attended a couple of windmill-fixing episodes and that was plenty.

With great effort, Slim pointed his bony frame toward the barn and began walking. At the entrance, he glanced back at me and winked. "Watch this." He turned toward the barn door and yelled out, "Loper, I just have a feeling this is going to be a wonderful day." He flinched, waiting for the thunder and lightning.

It came. Inside the barn, Loper's voice boomed, "Slim, when you get fired from this job, which could happen any day now, you can go into preaching full-time. Until then, please dry up and try to make yourself useful!"

Slim chuckled and shuffled into the barn, and for the next ten minutes, the air was filled with the sounds of clanging and banging as the men gathered up their tools. They made three trips from the barn to the pickup, lugging ropes and cables and heavy boxes of windmill parts.

Slim was still trying to make conversation. "Loper, do you know how many cowboys it takes to screw in a lightbulb?"

"No."

"You'll love this. It takes four—one to hold the lightbulb and three to turn the house. Heh."

Loper dumped his load onto the pickup's flatbed, jerked a red bandana out of his hip pocket, and . . . this was pretty amazing . . . stuffed the two ends of the rag into his ears. He gave Slim a fanged smile and went back into the barn for another load.

Slim dumped his tools onto the flatbed and shrugged. "I always liked that joke. It's the only one I could ever remember."

Moving at his usual pace (slow motion), Slim went sludging back into the barn. At that very moment, who should come walking up but Little Alfred, my most favorite pal in the whole world. On a normal day, I would have leaped to my feet and given him a few licks on the face, but today . . . I, uh, whapped my tail on the ground and called it good.

"Hi, Hankie. It's kind of hot, isn't it?"

Right. Very hot.

Slim and Loper came blundering out of the barn again, loaded down with gear. Alfred said, "Hi, Dad." Loper didn't hear, so the boy tried again, in a louder voice. "Hi, Dad!" Alfred looked closer at his dad. "He's got a rag in his ears!"

Slim said, "Don't pay him any mind, Button. He's on a crusade to make this the worst day since the volcano went off at Palm Play. I tried to cheer him up with one of my best jokes but it only confused him."

Alfred went to his dad and tugged on his pant leg. "Hey, Dad, you've got something in your ears."

Loper looked down at him. "What?" He uncorked one of his ears. "Oh, hi, son."

"How come you've got a rag in your ears?"

"I'm trying to gather up windmill tools, and I can't concentrate with all the noise." He jerked his head toward Slim. Slim stuck out his tongue and made a sour face.

Alfred brightened. "Can I go wiff ya'll and help?"

Loper patted him on the head. "Not this time, son. It's not likely to be much fun."

Slim muttered, "We can bet on that."

Loper shot him a dark glare. "Well, we're burning daylight. Let's get this over with."

They loaded into the pickup, and Loper started the engine. Over the noise, we heard Slim say, "Loper, you know the trouble with you?"

"Of course I do. Poor help." Then Loper turned up the volume on the radio, and they roared away.

Little Alfred drifted over to us. "Hi, doggies. Want to play?"

I gave him a wooden stare. Play?

"We could play Chase the Ball."

Ha ha.

"We could go exploring. Want to do that?"

Exploring? I wanted to explore the inside of an ice-cold watermelon and stay there until the first snow of the season. Other than that, no thanks.

He pushed out his lower lip at me. "Come on, Hankie, you're no fun."

Right. Sometimes that bothered me and sometimes it didn't. Right now, I just didn't give a rip.

He made an ugly face at me and started down to the house. "You're just a lazy bum."

Exactly, and proud of it, too. Okay, I wasn't proud of it. Being a lazy bum was nothing to be proud of but I couldn't help myself, not in this heat.

Ho hum. Time crawled by. Half an hour later, we heard sounds of life down at the house. A door slammed. Someone had come outside. With great effort, I swung my head around and saw Sally May standing in the yard, spraying her flowers and shrubberies with the water hose.

"Drover, Sally May has come out of the house. One of us needs to go down to the yard gate and give her a greeting."

"How come?"

"Because that's what we do. It's part of our job. When our people come outside, we're supposed to greet them. Dogs have been doing it for thousands of years."

"No wonder I'm so tired."

"What?"

"I said . . . I'll be derned. Which one of us will do it this time?"

I pondered that for a moment." Actually, I was wondering if you might take it, Drover. It wouldn't have to be anything fancy or special."

"What would I have to do?"

"Not much, just our basic Howdy Routine— chug down to the gate, give her some wags and a smile, tell her that you care deeply about her life, and come right back. It would be an easy way for you to build up some points."

"I guess I could use the points."

"Exactly. It never hurts to build up a few extra points with Sally May."

"Yeah, but I have a problem."

I rolled my eyes. "All right, Drover, tell me about the problem."

"Well, I hate to admit it. You'd probably think I'm a louse if you knew the truth."

"That's a risk we'll have to take, I suppose. What's the truth, and hurry up."

"Well . . ." He glanced over both shoulders and whispered, "I really don't care deeply about her life."

I stared at the runt. "What? You really don't . . . Drover, what kind of dog are you? I'm shocked and astamished that you'd even say such a thing."

"See? I knew it! I never should have told you the truth, but it's true. I just don't care deeply about her life, not today."

I took a breath of air and tried to absorb this astounding rulevation . . . revulation . . . revolution . . . I was shocked. "When did this start? When did you first notice it?"

"Well . . . about thirty minutes ago. I think it has something to do with the heat. I just don't give a rip about anything, and I don't think I can care deeply about her life right now."

"What about last evening when it was cooler?"

"Oh yeah, I cared back then, but now . . . I just don't think I could pull it off. It would be a big fat lie."

"Hmmm. This is serious, Drover. It cuts to the very heart of what we are as dogs. I mean, if a dog doesn't have deep feelings about his own people, what's left?"

"I don't know. Four legs and a stub tail, I guess."

"That's not much." I jacked myself up off the ground. "All right, son, I'll take this one, but I'm warning you. If we don't see some improvement in your attitude, we'll have to take some drastic measures."

He gave me a sad look. "Thanks, Hank. I'll do better when the weather cools down, I promise."

CHAPTER THREE

Sally May's Oasis

I left him lying in the shade. Just imagine, a dog that didn't care about the lady of the house, the very lady who fed us scraps! What was the world coming to?

Oh well. I tried to forget the sorry state of the world and made my way down the dusty dog trail to the yard gate. I could feel the sun baking the hairs on my back. My mouth was parched and dry.

But in spite of it all, I marched to the gate, sat down in front of Sally May, and launched myself into the Howdy Program—switched the tail circuits over to Broad Caring Sweeps, went to Bright Lights on the eyes, and squeezed up a smile of Utter Sincerity.

"Why, Sally May! I see you've come out of the house and you're watering your shrubberies. I haven't seen you in several hours and I just wanted you to know how deeply I care about..."

What a pack of lies! I couldn't go on with it. I flopped down on the ground. The Caring Wags came to a sudden stop. The Bright Lights went out in my eyes, and I found myself staring at the dusty ground.

Who could care about anything in this heat? I had thought that I could pull it off, that all my years of training and discipline would get me through the routine, but the awful heat had dragged me down.

I turned a pair of glazed eyes toward Sally May. She saw me and smiled. "Hello, Hank. It's hot, isn't it?"

Yes ma'am, it was hot. Furthermore, I didn't give a rip about . . .

I noticed a cool breeze blowing across the yard and into my face. It felt good . . . wonderful. At last, something cool and refreshing! It was the water, see, the wind blowing across the spray of Sally May's water. And then I noticed that everything inside the fence was GREEN—as green and refreshing as green refreshing greenery.

Wow!

I mean, the whole world was baked to a crisp and shriveled up in the heat, but that little oasis in Sally May's yard . . .

Hmmmm.

I, uh, returned to the control room of my mind and began reprogramming the program: up on all-fours, Broad Caring Wags, Bright Lights in the eyes, big cowdog smile . . .

I stood up and smiled. "Why, Sally May, how nice to see you again! I'm here to deliver a very special message and to let you know that, well, I care DEEPLY about your life. No kidding. How are the children? How's your day been going?"

At this point, I hooked my front paws over the top of the fence and mushed on with my presentation. "Oh, and by the way, I was just noticing your yard—admiring it, actually. It's so . . . well, cool and damp and fresh, and I was wondering..."

You might find this part hard to believe, but here goes. I slithered myself over the fence and oozed down into the cool, green refreshingness of the grass. Pretty amazing, huh? You bet. And even more amazing was that I did it with Maximum Stealth, so quietly and cunningly that she didn't even notice.

Heh heh.

Which meant that . . . well, she would probably

24

think that I'd been there all the time. No invasion of her precious yard by dogs, no big deal. We were just there, she and I, chatting and laughing about our various lives and sharing precious moments of . . . something. Preciousness.

And *caring* about each other. That was the most impointant pork. *We cared deeply about each other's lives.*

Once inside the yard, I resumed my presentation. "Sally May, I can hardly express how deeply and sincerely I admire you for . . . well, for all the things you do. There are so many things a dog can admire in you that I'm . . . well, ha ha, who could list them all?"

Was it selling? I studied her carefully. It was hard to tell. Slowly, very slowly, her gaze swung around and locked on me. I swallowed hard. The moment of truth had arrived.

She said, "You're in my yard."

Uh . . . yes, that was true.

I waited for more, but that's all she said. Her gaze returned to the flower beds, and I was left to desiphon the meaning of her words. See, I knew she had some strong opinions about Dogs in the Yard (she didn't allow it), yet there I was in her yard and . . . well, she hadn't screeched or chased me with a broom or anything.

This seemed pretty strong proof that my program was working. Her heart was beginning to soften and I needed to press on with my presentation. I had already picked out the spot where I wanted to ... well, spend some time: the iris patch on the north side of the house, which appeared to be the very coolest spot on the ranch—out of the sun, out of the dusty wind, great location.

Oh, and it also happened to be the favorite loafing spot of Pete the Barncat, which made it even more inviting. (Of course, Pete would have to vacate the property when I took it over.)

But I didn't dare make my move to the iris patch, not yet. That would be too sudden, too abrupt. Before I moved into the iris patch, so to speak, I needed to do a little more ... how can I say this? A little more "diplomatic work" with Sally May.

Charm her. Win her heart. Convince her that I *belonged* in her yard.

I switched all systems over to Heavy Charm and went back to work. Here's the message I beamed to her:

"Sally May, words and tail wags can hardly express my deep and sincere admiration for the fine work you've done in your yard. Did you, uh, do all this landscraping yourself? You have such an eye for beauty! Every little shrubbery and blade of grass is just, well, perfect. So green, so cool, so inviting. Terrific.

"And . . . well, maybe you've noticed that it's very hot today, and maybe you've noticed that I'm wearing a fur coat. Perhaps you've even been worried about me. I mean, everyone knows that you're the kind of lady who worries about her pets and animals, and let me say right here that I've always admired that quality in you—the fact that you CARE so much about animals and doing the right thing."

I held my breath and waited. Her eyes swung around again. And she said, "You're still in my yard."

That didn't sound so good, but let me point out that she said it with a smile. Hey, this was going pretty well, and it was time to make a dash for the Bottom Line.

"Yes, Sally May, and speaking of the yard, let me take this opportunity to express some thoughts and feelings that are . . . well, close to my heart. I know we've gone through some rocky times, you and I, and we've had our share of . . . well, misunderstandings. Missed opportunities. Failures to communicate our, uh, deepest feelings about each other.

"I'll admit that I've made a few . . . that is, a few mistakes have been made, and I know that they've damaged our relationship. Sometimes I've even had the feeling that . . . well, you don't trust me. In your yard, for example. And this has really bothered me. Deeply. No kidding.

"But I want you to know that I'm a changed dog. An older dog. A wiser and more mature dog. And I feel that our relationship has progressed to the point where you can trust me in your yard, trust me to do the right thing, to care for all your precious little flowers and shrubberies and blades of grass.

"Anyway, it's hotter than blue blazes today, and since you care so much about the, uh, welfare of animals and helpless creatures and so forth I was wondering . . . hey, what would you think if I moved into the yard for a couple of days? Huh?"

I beamed her my broadest and most sincere smile. She studied me for a long moment, and I had a feeling that the ice in her heart was beginning to melt. Any second now, she would . . .

HUH?

What happened next almost broke my heart. I mean, after all the time and care I had poured into my presentation . . .

Here's what happened. She said, "Hank, you know the rules. No dogs in the yard."

Yes, but I was wondering . . .

"Hank . . . out!"

Sure, but maybe this time we could . . .

And then she . . . SHE SPRAYED ME WITH THE GARDEN HOSE!

Okay, fine, if that's the way she felt about it. If I wasn't welcome in her yard, I would just . . .

Battered and wounded by the piercing spray of the garden hose, I made a dash to the fence and went sailing over the top. Safe on the other side, I paused long enough to beam her a look we call "My Life Is Ruined and You're the Cause." It's a facial expression we save back for the very darkest moments, and it should have caused her to . . . I don't know, cry or feel awful or something.

But I guess it didn't work, because she chirped a little laugh and said, "Hank, I'm sorry, but what can I do? You don't take hints, and I'm *not* going to let you trample and dig up my yard. Period." She turned off the water hydrant and started toward the house. At the door, she turned and said, "Stay out of my yard."

Those words cut me to the crick. After all the time I'd spent trying to win her heart and con-

vince her . . . what does it take to please these women? What does a dog have to do to convince them that . . .

Suddenly I had to face the crushing reality that my presentation—my very best and most sincere presentation—had fallen into the dust like a...something. A crippled buzzard. A wounded goose. A ruptured duck.

I had opened my heart to her, exposed my deepest and most secret feelings, and she had washed them all away with one splat of the garden hose. I was so wounded and damaged, I wasn't sure I would ever . . .

Oh well. It had been a long shot anyway. Sally May had always been a tough sell, so getting the bum's rush from her wasn't exactly the biggest surprise in the world. And getting sprayed with water had felt pretty good.

Huh?

A cat was standing on the other side of the fence, grinning at me and flicking the end of his tail back and forth.

CHAPTER FOUR

A Conversation
with the Cat

It was Pete the Barncat—who, for your information, never spent any time catching mice in the barn or anywhere else. He spent his whole life lounging in the shade of the iris patch and making a nuisance of himself.

Have we discussed cats? Maybe not. I don't like 'em, never have. And the cat I dislike the most in the whole world is Pete, who has some kind of genius for showing up at the very worst of times.

Such as now. And there he was, giving me that simpering grin that drives me nuts. "Hi, Hankie. Did you get sprayed?"

I gave the little snot a withering glare and marched away. He probably thought he could provoke me into a childish display of temper. Ha!

The foolish cat. Little did he know that I was a very busy dog and had more important . . .

On second thought . . . I whirled around and marched back to the fence. "What did you just say?"

"I said," he grinned and blinked his eyes, "you got sprayed."

"That's correct, kitty, I got sprayed. Perhaps you think that's funny."

He snickered. "Yes, yes, it was very funny. You should have seen that look on your face when she . . . hee hee . . . turned the hose on you!"

I felt my lips curling up into a snarl, but I caught it just in time and turned it into a calm, pleasant smile. See, I knew what the cat was trying to do: provoke me into an "incident," let us say, right there in front of Sally May, which would get me into even more and deeper trouble with the Lady of the House.

But I knew Pete's tricks and I wasn't going to fall for this one. I beamed him a sweet smile and said, "You're right, Pete, I got sprayed, but I *wanted* to get sprayed. That's why I went into the yard, so that Sally May could cool me down with a nice little shower of water."

"Oh really?"

"That's correct. Why else would I have gone into the yard? It was part of a clever plan, Pete, and as you can see, it worked to perfection. See? I'm wet, cool, and refreshed."

"Hankie, I think," he began purring and rubbing on the fence, "you're jealous because I get to stay in the yard, and you don't."

"No, not at all."

"And it just eats your liver that I'm Sally May's special pet."

"Nothing could be further from the truth. For your information, Sally May and I have enjoyed a wonderful relationship."

"Then," he fluttered his eyelids and grinned, "why did she order you out of the yard? Hmmm? See, I'm in the yard and, look, you're not/Stick your head in a coffee pot/Bring it out, red hot. And that says it all, Hankie. I spend my days in the iris patch, and you have to live out there in the heat and the dust. Poor doggie!"

I struggled to control my savage instincts. "You're trying to get me stirred up, aren't you?"

"Um-hm. Is it working?"

"Not even close. You must be slipping."

"Oh really? Well, what if I . . . hissed at you?"

"I don't know, Pete. Try it and we'll see what happens."

He arched his back, widened his yellowish eyes, and hissed at me. I watched him with a smile and—get this—gave no reaction at all. "Gosh, Pete, it didn't work. Try it again." He humped himself up and hissed even louder this time. I laughed in his face. "Sorry, Pete, the old magic just isn't there. Maybe it's the heat, or maybe . . . maybe your tricks aren't working any more, huh? What do you think?"

I could see that he was getting mad. "Hissing has always worked, Hankie. Something's going on here. What is it?"

I sat down and looked at his sour face. "Maybe I shouldn't tell you this, Pete, but what the heck? See, you've used that hissing trick too many times. I've figured it out, I know what you're trying to do. That chapter in our lives is over."

"I'm not convinced, Hankie."

"No? Then try it again." The cat glared at me and didn't hiss. I chuckled. "See, your problem is that you're too lazy to learn new tricks. We dogs learn from experience. When we see your same tired old tricks over and over, we figure them out. I mean, how dumb do you think I am?"

He stared at me with his big cattish eyes. "That's an interesting question, Hankie. I might want to think about it."

"Fine. You think about it all you want, but I can tell you the answer. I'm not dumb at all, and you're over the hill. The old stuff doesn't work any more. The world has passed you by."

"Oh really?"

"That's right. You belong in a museum, Pete, a museum for fat lazy cats who spend their lives loafing in the shade."

A secret grin spread across his mouth. "Bet you'd like to be in the shade, wouldn't you, Hankie?"

"Me? Ha ha. No, Pete, I . . . what makes you say that?"

"Because that's what you were trying to do when you sneaked into the yard. You wanted my iris patch, didn't you, hmmmmmm?"

I narrowed my eyes at the little sneak. "Don't be spreading lies about me, weasel. For your information, I care nothing about iris patches or shade. I love this heat. It makes me tougher and smarter. That's all I ever wanted to be, Pete, tough and smart."

"Oh really?" He rolled his eyes up at the sky. "What if I offered you a deal on my iris patch?"

"First, I'd laugh in your face. Then I'd walk away. Ha ha, good-bye." I whirled around and marched away. The dumb cat. Did he think I'd actually . . . I returned to the fence. "What did you mean, make a *deal* on the iris patch?"

36

He rolled over on his back and began playing with his tail. "Well, Hankie, maybe you're right. Maybe I'm getting fat and lazy and spending too much time loafing in the shade. The old tricks just don't work any more."

"Right, exactly my point, although . . . to be honest, Pete, I hardly know what to say. I mean, all these years we've been . . . you're admitting that I'm right? You, a cat?"

"Um-hm. It hurts, but facts are facts and truth is truth."

"Right. I've said that many times. But you said something about . . . a deal."

He nodded and whispered, "I'll rent you my iris patch for the rest of the day."

My ears leaped straight up. "You'll rent . . . what's the catch, Pete? Forgive me, but I don't exactly trust you."

"There's no catch. You can use my iris patch for one day, and I get first dibs on scraps for three days."

"That's your deal? Ha ha!" I whirled around and marched . . . back to the fence. "That's a crooked deal, Pete. One day in the shade for three days' scraps? It ought to be reversed, three days in the shade for one day's scraps."

He gave me an insolent smirk and licked his

paw. "That's my best offer, Hankie. Take it or leave it."

Suddenly I felt the hair rising on the back of my neck and heard a growl rumbling in the deep vicissitudes of my throat. In this awful heat, did I have enough energy to thrash a cheating little pipsqueak of a cat? Yes, by George! I rolled the muscles in my enormous shoulders and began rumbling toward the . . .

"Hank! Leave the cat alone!"

Huh? Leave the cat . . . where had that voice come from? I hit the brakes and turned my head toward the house. Oops. Sally May had just come out the door, and right behind her came Little Alfred.

I must admit that the sight of Sally May sent a shiver down my backbone, but right away, I could see that something unusual was going on. The clues were very plain to see. You want to see the List of Clues? I guess it wouldn't hurt to go public with this information. Here we go.

Secret Clue List #806-555-7611

Clue Number One: Sally May came out of the house, carrying a plastic pitcher and some paper cups.

Clue Number Two: Little Alfred seemed to be holding . . . was that a sign? Yes, it appeared to be a piece of cardboard with some kind of message written on one side: "Fresh Cold Lemonade $1.00."

Clue Number Three: Sally May said, "Well, this ought to keep you busy for a while. Stay out of the road, watch the traffic, and come back in one hour."

Clue Number Six: Little Alfred said, "Okay, Mom. Me and my doggies'll sell a whole bunch of lemonade."

Clue Number Seven: A deep scowl passed across Sally May's face, and she said, "Must you take the dogs? Oh, I guess it'll be all right, but watch them like a hawk and don't let them drink your lemonade. I squeezed those lemons by hand."

Clue Number Eight: Drover drifted down from the machine shed and joined me at the yard fence. Actually, that wasn't a clue and it didn't have much to do with anything, but it did happen, so I thought I would mention it.

**End of Secret Clue List
Please Destroy At Once!**

Do you see the meaning of this? Holy smokes, unless my ears were playing tricks on me, Little Alfred was fixing to go into the lemonade business . . . and he wanted to take me on as a partner!

I whirled around to the cat and gave him a worldly sneer. "Hey Pete, you know that deal we were discussing? I'm no longer interested in your iris patch. I have bigger flies to fish. So long, kitty."

And with that, I whirled away from the little cheat and marched straight to the yard gate. There, I met my business partner as he stepped out of the yard, carrying the pitcher in both hands and holding the sign under his arm.

The boy came out the gate, walking slowly so as not to spill his . . . whatever it was in the pitcher. He called out, "Come on, doggies, wet's go. We're gonna set up a lemonade stand and make some money!"

I shot a glance at my assistant. "Did you hear that? The lad is going to start a lemonade business and needs our help."

"I'll be derned."

"And it would be good, Drover, if you could show some excitement and enthusiasm."

"Yeah, but I'm fresh out of both."

"Then fake it. On your feet, son, we've got a job to do." He didn't move. "Drover, I know it's hot, but challenges like this give us a chance to show what we're made of."

"Yeah, but I already know: melted butter. I just don't think this leg would make it."

"Which leg?"

"Left rear." He stood up and limped around in a circle. "See?"

"It looks fine to me. Let's go."

"Oh, my leg! Oh, the pain! Oh, the heat!"

"Never mind, skip it, Drover. I'll go by myself."

I left him to his moaning and whining, and trotted in a northward direction until I caught up with Little Alfred. I went into the Raised Lips procedure and gave him a smile.

He returned the smile. "Hi, Hankie. Are you ready to sell some lemonade?"

Oh sure. I was ready to answer the call of duty, and if that meant helping my little pal sell lemonade on a hot day, so be it.

Besides, heh heh, I was kind of thirsty.

CHAPTER FIVE

Alfred and I Go into the Lemonade Business

As we hiked away from the house, Little Alfred and I launched ourselves into "The Lemonade Song." Have we ever done it before? Maybe not. Here's how it went.

The Lemonade Song
Yo-ho! Yo-ho! Yo-ho, yo-ho, yo-ho!

We're off to sell some lemonade, we know it's
    going to be fun.
We're off to launch a business deal, in spite of
    the broiling sun.
When the customers come, we'll peddle our
    stuff

While Drover and Kitty Cat sit on their duffs.
The world can't wait to buy 'em a cup.
This lemonade business is going to be fun.

We made our way north to the county road. There, Little Alfred hung his cardboard sign on the mailbox. Then he set the pitcher down on the edge of the road, and we waited for our customers to arrive.

We waited. And waited. Alfred scanned the horizon for a cloud of dust that would signal the approach of our first customer. No one was rushing up to buy our product, it appeared, so we sang another verse.

This summer sun is awfully hot, the sweat is
    starting to pour.
The county road is empty, and no one has
    come to our store.
Well, if nobody comes, then what shall we do?
We'll sit here and boil like venison stew.
Or maybe we'll have a drink or two.
This lemonade business is going to be fun.

The boy wiped a trickle of sweat off his forehead, sat down in the shade of the mailbox, and poured a cup of lemonade.

"Welp, I guess I'll try some myself." He leaned his head back and took a long swig. I watched. His eyes brightened and a smile bloomed on his mouth. "Boy, that's some good stuff. My mom sure makes tasty lemonade." He put the cup to his mouth and drained it.

I suddenly realized that my bodily parts had begun . . . my ears jumped into the Alert Position, my tail brushed across the ground, my tongue shot out of my mouth, and my front paws moved up and down.

It was almost as though I was . . . well, thirsty and craving a drink of something wet and cool.

Alfred noticed. "You want a dwink, Hankie?"

Oh no, I wouldn't want to be a burden and we probably needed to save the lemonade for the, uh, customers . . . but on the other hand . . . gee, come to think of it, I'd never tasted lemonade before. Was it, uh, pretty tasty?

I licked my lips, swept my tail across the ground, and waited to see what would happen.

He refilled the cup and held it under my nose. "Here, Hankie. You need a dwink, 'cause it's awful hot."

Right, exactly, and what a friend! Didn't I tell you we were pals to the bone? Yes sir, the boy had a special understanding of what it was like, being a dog on a blazing hot summer day.

I initiated the Delicate Drink procedure and began lapping from the cup. It was a pretty small cup and fitting my tongue into that tiny opening proved to be no ball of wax, but I got 'er done. Lap, lap. Wow! The kid was right. His mother sure knew how to make . . .

Oops.

Maybe I got carried away and went a little too deep with my tongue. Or maybe I tried to fit my entire nose into the tiny paper cup. Anyway, it caused an accident. The cup slipped out of his hand and fell to the ground.

He scowled at the puddle of fresh lemonade spreading across the dusty ground. "Dwat. The cup's too little."

Right. The cup was entirely too small for the job, and it was nobody's fault that our attempts to restore my bodily fluids had ended in failure. On the other hand . . . uh . . . what about the pitcher? I mean, the pitcher was pretty big, right? It had a nice big opening at the top, if someone were to, uh, remove the lid, right?

I pointed my nose toward the pitcher and went to Slow Thumps on the tail section. Would the boy get the message? I held my breath and waited.

His eyes went from me to the pitcher and back to me, then back to the pitcher. He scowled and chewed his lip. Then he said, "I wonder if . . ."

Yes? Yes?

"Hankie, would you mind dwinking out of the pitcher?"

Me? Mind drinking . . . oh no, that would be fine. Why, any dog who'd turn down a drink from a pitcher would be too fussy for his own good, and this was not going to be a problem for us. In other words, could we, uh, pry the lid off that thing?

He pried off the lid and gave me a big smile. "Okay, Hankie, sit."

Sit? Hey, it was time to *drink*, and could we speed this up a bit? I mean, the taste of lemonade was still lingering in my mouth and . . . okay, he was working on manners and obedience, so I plunked myself down.

"Good doggie. On the count of three, I'll snap my fingers and you can dwink."

Got it, fine, you bet, count of three.

"One! Two!"

Tense and bursting with excitement, I waited for the third count. It didn't come. Instead, the boy turned his head to the east, toward the sound of an approaching vehicle. His finger froze in the air. "Oh goodie, somebody's coming."

47

Oh goodie, I was dying of thirst and . . . okay, maybe I should have waited for the command, but what's a poor dog to do? I mean, the boy had already given me permission to drink out of the pitcher, only he'd gotten distracted in the middle of his countdown. All at once, it seemed perfectly reasonable that I should . . .

I, uh, stuck my nose and face into the pitcher and began lapping like there was no tomorrow. LAP, LAP, LAP. I mean, I had a suspicion that this offer would soon expire, so to speak, since we had a potential customer . . . LAP, LAP, LAP . . . bearing down on us from the . . .

"Hankie, no! Don't dwink my lemonade, not now!"

LAP, LAP, LAP.

Okay, we had a little struggle. Alfred and I, that is. After giving me permission to drink out of the pitcher, he had suddenly . . . what can I say? He'd changed his mind, I suppose, but try to understand my side of the story.

It was hotter than blazes out there, right? And we'd both been out in the sun for hours and hours. Okay, for fifteen minutes. Alfred had taken *his* drink and he'd opened up the pitcher so that I could get mine, but then complications developed and he got sidetracked from the, uh, important issues of the moment.

I lapped and slurped, while he tugged and pulled. "Hankie, get out of my lemonade! You're gonna ruin my business." At last he managed to pull my face out of the pitcher and got the lid snapped back on. He wagged his finger at me and said, "No, no, no. That was naughty!"

Right. Okay, maybe it was naughty, and one side of my inner self recognized that being naughty wasn't nice. But the other side of my inner self was prepared to live with the guilt, because . . . hee hee . . . my outer self had managed to smuggle half of that delicious lemonade out of the pitcher, and to be real honest about it . . .

Wait a second. Maybe the kids shouldn't be hearing this. Let's back off and take another run at it.

Okay, here's my new position on Lemonade Smuggling, and I want all the kids to pay close attention. Lemonade Smuggling is wrong, naughty, uncouth, and unsanitary. Dogs should *never drink lemonade out of pitchers*, and kids should never allow their dogs to do it. Never, not under any circumstances, and especially when customers are coming into the store.

There. That's better, don't you think?

Anyway, the vehicle turned out to be a white Chevy pickup. As it approached, we finished the Lemonade Song.

We'll soon be getting a customer. We'll give
    him a wonderful pitch.
He'll order a glass and pay us a buck, and
    then we are going to be rich.
I think I'll buy me a baseball bat.
I'll buy me a mousetrap to use on the cat.
We're happy as hogs and now we know that
This lemonade business is sure lots of fun.

Little Alfred stood up, waved toward the pickup, and pointed to his sign. The pickup drove past, then stopped. The driver put it in reverse and backed up.

Alfred and I traded long glances, and he whispered, "Uh-oh. Should we tell him?"

I looked deeply into my soul for the answer. It was one of the most difficult moral decisions of my whole career. Suddenly the answer came to me, like a whispered voice from the deep. With innocent looks and slow wags on the tail section, I replied: "I didn't see a thing, how about you?"

Alfred gave me a little grin. "I think we won't tell anyone. It'll be our secret, Hankie."

Right. Good decision. Great idea. We didn't know anything about anything, and besides, nothing had happened anyway.

A man stepped out of the pickup and came toward our lemonade stand.

CHAPTER SIX

Our Very First Customer

I knew right away that this guy didn't live in our neighborhood, because he was dressed in safari clothes. What are safari clothes? Khaki pants and shirt and a wide-brimmed hat. They weren't cowboy clothes, and this guy looked different.

Oh, and did I mention that he had a several days' growth of beard on his cheeks and chin? He did, and if he hadn't had such a pleasant face, I might have growled at him.

The stranger walked up to Little Alfred and gave him a smile. "Hi there, son. You're selling lemonade?"

"Yes sir."

The man extended his hand. "David Wilkens. I'm an archeologist."

Alfred shook his hand. "I'm Alfred and this is my dog, Hank. What's an arkimolgist?"

"Well, I study things that are very old: tools made of flint, prehistoric houses and storage pits, clay pottery, shell beads, bones, things like that."

Bones? My ears shot up. All at once, I was interested in this conversation.

Little Alfred dug his hand into his pocket and came up holding something in his fingers. "I have an arrowhead. My dad found it yesterday."

Mr. Wilkens slipped a pair of glasses on his nose and studied the arrowhead, turning it around in his fingers. "It's a nice little Washita point from the Plains Village period, made of good-quality Alibates flint. It's eight or nine hundred years old."

"Older than my dad?"

Mr. Wilkens laughed. "Well, I haven't met your dad, but I'd say so, yes. Now, here's what I want you to do, Alfred. I want you to put this in a plastic bag and tell your dad to record the location where he found it on a piece of paper, and keep them together. An artifact without site information is no good to anyone. Can you do that?"

"Yes sir."

"Good. When your dad finds another artifact in that location, he can put it in the same bag, and one of these days, when I come back and ask to see your collection, you'll have some information I can use."

"Is arkimology fun?"

Mr. Wilkens tugged on his chin. "It's fun if you're curious about the past, but it involves a lot of hard work."

Alfred showed off the muscle in his right arm. "I bet I could do it. I'm pwetty stwong."

"I'll bet you are. Maybe your mother can bring you over to the site and we'll put you to work screening dirt." He glanced down at the pitcher. "You got any lemonade left?"

"Yes sir. You're our first customer."

Mr. Wilkens peered into the pitcher. "It's only half-full. What happened to the rest of it?"

Oops. Alfred's gaze slid around to me and his eyes seemed to be asking, "What do I say now?"

With my eyes, I sent back a reply. "If you want to lose a customer, tell him your dog drank out of it. If you don't want to kill the business . . . how can I say this? Tell him a tiny falsehood—not a big whopper, mind you, but a tiny restructuring of the truth, let us say."

The lad got the message and gave me a secret

grin. He turned back to Mr. Wilkens. "Oh, I got thirsty and took a dwink."

There we go! Just right. Not a huge whopper but a slight restructuring of the facts. Alfred gave me a wink and I winked back. Heh heh. We had dodged a bullet. Pretty clever, huh? You bet.

Mr. Wilkens continued to study the pitcher. "You must have been pretty thirsty."

"Sir?"

"It's a two-quart pitcher. If it's half-empty, it means you drank a quart of lemonade. I'm surprised your stomach could hold a quart." He narrowed his eyes and looked at Alfred's stomach. "And your abdomen doesn't appear to be distended."

Alfred's smile vanished. "Well, I . . . I . . . I . . . I . . ."

"Maybe you spilled some of it."

"Yes sir, that's it. I almost forgot."

"Or . . . " Suddenly, with no warning, his eyes swung around and . . . yipes . . . came at me like bullets. ". . . maybe someone else took a drink."

Me? Hey, I knew nothing about this deal, almost nothing at all. And besides, dogs don't drink lemonade. We drink water, plain water. Honest.

There was a long throbbing moment of

silence. Then Alfred gave me an elbow in the ribs. "Hankie, see what you did! Now you've ruined my business!" The boy swallowed hard and looked up at Mr. Wilkens. "My dog stuck his head into the pitcher and . . ." He covered his face with his hands. "I told you a big fat lie and now I can't sell you any lemonade!"

Alfred hid his face and I squirmed, as our new business went sliding toward the brink of bankrubble. I felt terrible, but don't forget who'd told the fib. It wasn't me. Okay, maybe I . . . never mind.

Alfred peeked out between his fingers. "How did you know?"

"Your dog has drops of lemonade on his face."

Huh? Drops? I sent the old tongue out to, uh, mop up the evidence. Slurp.

Mr. Wilkens looked off in the distance. "There's a lesson here, Alfred. Two lessons, actually. Lesson One: Never tell a lie. It'll always come back to bite you. Lesson Two: If you just *have* to tell a windy tale, don't tell it to a professional archeologist. Do you know why?"

"No sir."

"Because, my boy, we are detectives. We have to draw conclusions from tiny bits of evidence, and very little escapes our notice."

Alfred nodded. "I'm sorry."

The man gave him a hard look. "Are you sorry that you got caught or sorry that you told a fib?"

"I'm sorry I told a fib."

Mr. Wilkens clapped his hands together. "Good, that settles it. Now we can get on with our business. I'll take the rest of your lemonade."

Alfred dropped his hands and stared at him. "But my dog . . ."

"Son, in this heat, I wouldn't care if your dog took a bath in it, as long as it's wet and cold." He went to his pickup and came back with a thermos bottle. "Fill 'er up. What do I owe you?"

"You can just have it for free."

Mr. Wilkens reached for his wallet and came out with a bill. "How about five bucks? Will that cover your expenses?"

Alfred's eyes almost popped out of his head. "Five bucks! Hankie, we're rich!" The boy took the money and waved it in the air.

That was good news, all right. We'd saved the business and made a fortune in the lemonade market, but all at once I had lost interest in sudden wealth. You know why? Because my gaze had wandered over to the back of Mr. Wilkens' pickup, and there, to my complete astonishment, I saw . . . you won't believe this part, so hang on . . . I saw the most gorgeous lady dog I'd seen in weeks. Months. Years. My whole life.

We're talking about killer good looks, drop-dead good looks. Golden hair. Long dignified nose. Proud head. Deep brown eyes. Ears that seemed to flow like a frozen waterfall of sorghum syrup.

WOW! You talk about eyes bugging out of your head! Fellers, my eyes popped out so far, I had to grab 'em out of the air and stuff 'em back where they belonged.

Don't get me wrong. I'm not the kind of dog who gets silly about the ladies, but this gal appeared to be something special and all at once, I lost all interest in the lemonade business. See, she was standing up in the back of the pickup and I was pretty sure that she was looking at . . . well, at ME, might as well come out and say it.

In fact, she appeared to be *staring* at me, and we're talking about eyes that shouted, "Oh dear, oh me, oh my! I'm looking at the handsomest, bravest dog in all of Texas!"

Well, what can I say? I don't go around advertising my charms, but she'd picked them up right away. In addition to being beautiful, she was obviously very intelligent. I needed to check this out.

CHAPTER SEVEN

I Charm a Lady Dog
from Boston

I slipped away from the store and swaggered my big bad self over to the pickup. I didn't speak right away. Instead, I marched around the pickup three times, sniffing the tires and, you know, giving her a chance to notice . . . well, my long cowdog nose, the rippling muscles in my enormous shoulders, the proud angle of my tail . . .

After giving her a few minutes to check out the goods, so to speak, I stopped and let my eyes drift up to her. Then, in my most startling voice, I delivered my opening line. "Hi there."

This seemed to take her breath away, but she managed to say, "Hi."

"You, uh, live around here?"

"Austin."

"That's up north, right?"

"South."

"I'd be the last one to argue with a lady, but I'm pretty sure it's north of here."

"It's south."

"Well, then, how do you explain all those lobsters?"

"What are you talking about?"

"Lobsters, ma'am. Austin is famous for its lobsters, and it's common knowledge that lobsters live in cold northern waters. Therefore, you can't possibly live south of here. I'm sorry to be so blunt but, well, facts are facts."

"We don't have lobsters in Austin."

I had to chuckle. "Well, you might never have seen them unless you did a lot of exploring on the seashore."

"We don't have a seashore."

"Of course you do. Austin is a very old and famous port city. Maybe you seen the sawshore but didn't recognize it."

"Excuse me?"

"I said, maybe you shaw the she sore . . . maybe you saw the she shore . . . maybe you saw the seashore but didn't recognize it. She shores have lots of water, sand, seaweed, jellyfish, and lobsters. Lobsters are red and have pinchers. Does any of that sound familiar?"

She took a slow breath of air. "Maybe you're thinking of Boston. I live in *Austin*. Austin is in Texas."

"It is?"

"Austin is the capital of Texas. It's exactly five hundred and fifty miles south of here."

"No kidding? And you don't have lobsters in Austin?"

She leaned toward me and, well, she seemed a little peeved. *"We do not have lobsters."*

I paced a few steps away and tried to gather my thoughts. "Ma'am, it's becoming clear that we've gotten some bad information. This happens all the time. Our enemies are constantly trying to confuse us by planting corrupted data into our systems, so let me give you an update." I whirled around and faced her. "Austin and Boston are two different places, even though their names rhyme, and you can forget about the Lobster Report. That was bogus information."

She stared at me for a long moment. "Who are you?"

Heh heh. This was going great. Already she was begging to know my name.

I gave her a bow wow. Wait, let me rephrase that. I gave her a *bow*, and wow, this was getting very interesting.

"I figured you'd get around to my name. Heh heh. Hank the Cowdog, ma'am, Head of Ranch Security. You're on my ranch and you have nothing to fear. You're my guest and I'll do everything in my power to make sure that your stay is safe and comfortable."

"Oh. Thanks."

"Think nothing of it, but now I must ask you a few questions." I leaned in her direction, dropped my voice to a raspy whisper, and wiggled my eyebrows. "What's your name?"

"Saffron."

"My goodness, I've known thousands of lady dogs but I've never met one named . . . what was it again?"

"Saffron. Saff-ron."

"Right. I've known Suzies and Saras and Sallies, but never a . . . what was it?"

"Saffron!"

"There we go. What kind of name is that?"

"I have no idea."

I figured this might be a good time to inject a little humor, so I said, "It doesn't mean 'lobster,' does it? Ha ha."

Yipes, maybe that was the wrong thing to say. Her nostrils flared out. "Will you please stop talking about lobsters!"

"Okay, sorry. I was just . . . look, you have to admit that it's an unusual name."

She shrugged. "I'm from Austin. What do you expect? Well, it was nice meeting you."

"I beg your pardon?"

"I thought you were leaving."

"Ha ha. Not at all, my lovely daffodil. This is your lucky day. I've got all the time in the world."

"Oh great."

I glanced over both shoulders. "What would you think if I, uh, leaped up into the pickup and sat beside you, hmm?"

Her gaze drifted toward the horizon. "To be perfectly honest, I'm not sure what I would think."

"But it might be pretty exciting, huh? Maybe we ought to give it a try." I went into the Deep Crouch Position and sprang upward with a mighty burst of . . . didn't quite make it over the tailgate, but I'm no quitter. I hooked my front paws over the top and shifted both back legs into Scramble gear. "Don't worry, I'll be there in just a second."

"If you scratch my boss's pickup . . ."

"Here I come!" It would have been better if I hadn't landed on top of her head. I knew that, but

I went flying over the tailgate and . . . well, there she was. BAM! "Oops, sorry. Here, let me help you up."

She pushed me away. "Oaf! You almost broke my neck!" She picked herself off the floor and staggered toward the front. The thought that I had caused her some pain touched my heart and I rushed to her side. "Here, let me . . ."

"AAAAAAA! Get off my tail!"

"Did I step on your tail?"

"Yes, you stepped on my tail!"

"Ma'am, I'm terribly sorry, but I was so concerned about your neck . . ."

"Get off my foot!"

"Me? I stepped on your foot?"

She backed herself into a corner and held up one paw. "Please! I'm fine, don't try to help, don't do anything. Just stay back." She rolled her head around. Crack, pop, snap.

"How's the neck?"

"It's fine, everything's fine."

"What a relief! You know, I landed pretty hard on top of your head."

"No kidding?"

"Oh yes, I'm a big guy and I had some momentum built up. Listen, how about a poem?"

She stared at me. "What?"

"A poem. You know, sometimes when we're not feeling our best, a poem can lift our spirits. And, well, I'm a pretty awesome poet."

"Maybe some other time."

"Okay, how about a few tricks? You ever see a dog do a back flip with a half-twist?"

She rolled another kink out of her neck. "Listen, I know you mean well, but I really don't have time for this. We're doing an excavation at the lake and we need to get back to the site."

"You do arkansology? Wow, what a coincidence! You won't believe this, my little sweet pea, but I am a genius at bones, and here's a great idea." I moved toward her.

"No, please, don't come any closer."

"Right, sorry. Anyway, I just had the greatest idea and you're going to love this. How's about if I . . ."

"Hankie? Here Hankie, come on!"

Huh? My ears had just picked up a message from Little Alfred, calling me back on duty. What lousy luck. I heaved a sigh and turned toward the lady of my dreams. "Ma'am, I have some terrible news. My outfit has just been reactivated. I must go."

"Good-bye."

"I know, I hate it, too, but when you're Head of Ranch Security, you march to the drum of a different beet. But I want you to know that this time we've spent together has caused my heart to soar."

"Right. I'm sore all over."

"Exactly, but this won't be our last time together. I have a feeling that we'll meet again."

Wearing a cute little smile, she came to me and touched my cheek, causing a flash of electrical current to course through my entire body. Then, in a soft whisper, she said, "You know what? I have a feeling that we *won't*."

My heart banged inside my chest as I moved closer and looked into the depths of her eyes. "My dearest, if it's the last thing I ever do . . ."

"Get off my foot!"

Alfred's voice tore through the silence. "Hankie, come on! Here, boy!"

I snapped to attention. "They're calling me and I must leave, but I shall find you again, oh beloved, if it's the last . . ."

"Good-bye."

". . . thing I ever do. Until we meet again . . . good-bye, Sardina!"

I leaped out of the back of the pickup before

she could call me back, before my heart could break into a hundred pieces. I mean, you talk about a sad farewell! It was a ripper and I didn't dare look back. Why, the sight of her sobbing might have . . . I couldn't even allow myself to think about it.

CHAPTER EIGHT

A New Assignment

~~~~~~

Pretty emotional scene, huh? You bet. I'm not the kind of dog who loses his head around the womenfolk, but this gal had turned me wrong-side out, upside-down, backward, and every which way but loose.

Who could forget those first words she'd said to me, as we looked into each other's eyes: "Hi." I would keep those words—well, that one word— forever locked away in the little cigar box of my heart.

But I had been called back into service, and I had to put all those perfumed memories behind me. Holding my head at a stern professional angle, I marched away from the sobs of my Newly

Beloved and set a course that would take me straight to Little Alfred.

He was still standing beside the mailbox, beside Mr. Wilcox . . . Williams . . . whatever he called himself . . . Wilkens, there we go, Mr. Wilkens . . . and his eyes were shining with delight. Alfred's eyes were shining with delight, that is. Mr. Wilkens' eyes were . . . why was he staring at ME? Hey, I had washed my face and removed all traces of the lemonade, so maybe he could stare at somebody else for a while.

Make one little mistake around here and they never let you forget it.

I marched up to my little pal and gave him a stiff salute. "Reporting for duty, sir."

The boy seemed breathless with excitement. "Hankie, I get to go over to the lake and help Mr. Wilkens dig up an old house! We're going to camp out and sleep in a tent!"

Mr. Wilkens smiled. "Now, slow down, son. This is still in the planning stage. We have to get your mother's permission and she might have other things for you to do. Let's drive down to the house and see what she says."

They loaded Alfred's stuff into the pickup, and I marched around to the rear of the pickup and prepared to leap into the back. Huh? They drove off without me.

You know, a lot of dogs would have gotten their feelings hurt, but I didn't give it a thought. Okay, I gave it a thought, one small thought, and decided, what the heck, they were busy and excited and just forgot to invite me. They probably knew that a big strapping dog like myself would have no problem walking a quarter mile to the house, even in the scalding heat, and they were sure right about that.

No problem. Besides, I was looking forward to having a few moments to myself, because I had a lot of things on my mind. Obviously, my career was about to take a major turn in a new and exciting direction, and I needed some time to make plans and chart a course for the future. I had no idea how long I would be digging bones with Mr. Wilkens and Alfred, and they were leaving me very little time to put my affairs in order before we shipped out.

I needed some time alone, is the point, but who or whom do you suppose came trotting up the road to meet me? Just the guy I didn't need or want to see. Drover.

He rushed up to me, all aflutter with excitement. "Oh my gosh, Hank, you'll never guess what I just saw in the back of that pickup!"

I kept walking. "You saw a gorgeous golden-haired lady dog."

The bottom fell out of his smile. "Oh drat, you saw her, too?"

"Of course I saw her, too. Her name is Sardina. She comes from Boston, our state capital. She works with an arkansologist and they dig up bones. She hates lobsters and has fallen madly in love with me. What else do you want to know about her?"

He gave me a tragic look then fell to the ground and began kicking all four legs. "I can't believe this. You cheated, and now my heart is broken! Oh, my heart!"

I glared down at the runt. "Drover, stop this childish display. You're embarrassing me."

"Yeah, but she smiled at me and there for a second, I thought . . . you stole her and it's no fair! Boo hoo!"

"Drover, I didn't steal her. To be honest, I had little or nothing to do with it. I merely said hello and, well, things happened so quickly, the two of us were just swept away."

"Yeah, and I've been swept away—into the garbage heap!"

"Son, I know how you must feel, but try to re-member that in the Game of Life, those who finish last are almost as important as those who finish first. The only difference is that if you finish last, you're a loser."

"Yeah, but she gave me the sweetest smile I ever saw."

"She was probably studying your bones and thought they looked funny."

He wiped a tear from his eye. "What's wrong with my bones?"

"Do you want the truth? Your bones are bony."

He started sniffling again. "You never told me that before."

"Well, you never asked, but it's very plain to see. You have the boniest bones I've ever seen, and I guess Sardina thought so, too. That's why she smiled. I'm sorry, but there you are."

"I can't take any more! First it was the stub tail and now this!" He blubbered and boo-hooed some more, then dried his eyes. "What kind of name is that?"

"Bony is not a name. It's a distractive itcha-tive."

"What?"

"I said, it's a destructive adjective. *Bony* de-scribes the boniness of a bone."

"No, I mean Sardina."

"Oh. Yes, it's an odd name, and I even told her so."

"It sounds like sardines."

"Well, she comes from a coastal city, somewhere down south. What's the capital of Texas?"

"Oklahoma?"

"No. Boston, that's it. She's from Boston."

"I thought Boston was the capital of Mackereloosus."

"Mackerels or sardines, they're all fish, Drover, and that's my whole point. Apparently the lady is fond of fish."

"Yeah, but you said she hates lobsters."

I stuck my nose in his face. "Lobsters are not fish. They have pinchers."

"Dentures?"

"What?"

"You said that lobsters wear false teeth."

"I did not say that lobsters wear false teeth! I said that dentures have pinchers and furthermore . . ." I blinked my eyes and glanced around. "Why are we discussing lobsters?"

"I don't know, I'm all confused."

I marched a few steps away and took a big gulp of fresh air. Suddenly I noticed that my

stomach was growling. "Drover, have you ever developed a craving for sardines?"

"Well, I ate a can of 'em once."

"Yes? How were they?"

"Well, they tasted like fish, only moreso."

"I see, yes. Well, this is very odd. All at once I feel this . . . this irrational craving for sardines."

"I'll be derned. You know, I'm kind of hungry for mackerel."

"Amazing. But why would two dogs in the Texas Panhandle be sitting around, thinking about fish?" For five long minutes, each of us was alone with his private thoughts. Then I heaved a sigh and returned to my companion. "Drover, I think it would be best if we kept this conversation to ourselves."

"Yeah, and I can't even remember what we were talking about."

I sat down beside him. "Me neither, and that worries me. I'm sure that we were discussing something important, but somehow we ended up talking about fish."

A tiny light of recognition flashed in Drover's eyes. "Wait, I almost forgot. I saw Pete down at the house. He said something you'll want to hear."

I heaved a sigh. "Very well, let's hear it and get it over with."

"He said . . . let me see if I can remember . . . I want to get it just right . . . he said . . . I think he said . . ."

"Drover, hurry up."

"Here we go. He said, 'Tell Hankie the weather's just perfect in my iris patch.' That's exactly what he said. Oh, and then he stuck out his tongue."

Those words went through me like a wooden nickel. "The little sneak stuck out his tongue?"

"Yep, he sure did. I saw it myself."

"One more question, Drover, and this could be crucial to the investigation. Did you feel that he intended the stuck-out tongue for you or for someone else?"

Drover rolled his eyes around. "Well, now that you mention it, I think maybe he meant it for . . . you."

I sprang to my feet and suddenly I could feel a gush of new energy flowing through the blood vessels of my arteries. "Just as I suspected! Behind my back, the little pest is sticking out his tongue at me. He doesn't have the guts to do it to my face."

"Yeah, so he did it to *my* face, and I ratted on him, hee hee."

I placed a paw on his shoulder. "It wasn't

ratting, son. You were just standing up for your comrades in the Security Division, and for that we are very grateful."

"Yeah, and it was fun, too. I love to rat on cats."

"Every dog with an ounce of decency loves to rat on cats. It's part of the wonder of being a dog. And now you know what the insolent cat has forced upon us."

"Yeah, hee hee, we're going to beat him up!"

"Exactly! *Do unto others, but don't take trash off the cats!* Come on, son, our unit is fixing to go into combat!"

"Oh goodie!"

Suddenly the morning air was filled with the growl of tank motors and the thud of marching feet, as the amassed forces of the entire Security Division moved like a deadly cloud toward ranch headquarters.

No one spoke. Every lip formed a tight determined line, and every eye was directed toward Ground Zero—the iris patch. Every soldier on this mission knew in his deepest heart that this would be the biggest and finalest showdown with our enemiest enemy, the sniveling, scheming little snot of a cat named Pete.

As our column rolled toward the house, I reached for the microphone of my mind. "Tank

One, this is Infantry One. How are things looking on your side? Over."

"Gosh, am I really a tank?"

"Roger that. How does it feel?"

"Well . . . pretty good, I guess. Reckon I ought to be making motor noise?"

"We've got a big ten-four on that, Tank One. You're cleared for motor noise. Give it your best shot, over."

"Brrrrrrrr brum brum, brrrrrr brum brum brum! How does that sound?"

"Five-by-five, Tank One. You're sounding good. Any sign of the enemy yet?"

"Well, let me look. Nope, I can't see Pete but . . . I'll be derned, there's a pickup parked in front of the house."

"Come back on that, Tank One, we've got a noisy line. Over."

"I said, there's a pickup parked beside the house, and . . . oh my gosh! Hank, I just remembered what we were talking about back there."

"Stick with the code names, son. I'm Infantry One. Repeat your message, over."

His breathless voice came over the sneakers. Speakers. "Back there, we were talking about something and we couldn't remember what it was. Remember?"

"Hurry up. Over."

I strained my ears to pick up his next transmission. "SARDINA!"

Huh?

All our tanks and armored vehicles stopped in their tracks. The tramp of thousands of marching feet fell silent. Our entire invasion force came to a halt on a hill overlooking the battle zone.

In the eerie silence, I spoke into the microphone. "Uh, Drover, you stay here with the troops. I'll go down and check this out."

ZOOM!

CHAPTER NINE

My New Career Gets Put On Hold

Maybe in all the excitement of the invasion, you missed the meaning of Drover's radio transmission, but I didn't. I heard it loud and clear, and let me see if I can explain it.

Okay, let's start with a well-known fact: Carrying on a normal conversation with Drover can rot your mind. In fact, there is no such thing as a normal conversation with Drover. Every conversation is totally abnormal, and sometimes it borders on chaos. The little mutt will take the thread of discussion and spin it into some kind of spiderweb, so that the unfortunate party on the other end begins to lose all contact with time, space, and reality.

I know what I'm talking about here. I've seen it

happen over and over. You start off talking about apples and you end up with oranges or pineapples. You start off talking about horses and before you know it, you're arguing about horseflies.

That is precisely what happened to our conversation at the mailbox. When it began, we were discussing one of the most important discoveries of my entire career, the lovely Miss Sardina Bandana of Boston, yet somehow Drover's power to corrupt all forms of communication had led us into . . .

This is embarrassing. I don't know how it happened. Somehow the little goof had steered our conversation into Pete the Barncat! Who wants to waste time talking about Pete or his iris patch resort? Not me, yet somehow it happened.

Oh well. The important thing is that I got it shut down only moments before our armored columns were scheduled to roll into ranch headquarters and make hamburger out of the cat. Don't get me wrong. Hamburgerizing the cat would have been fun but totally unnecessary, for you see, I NO LONGER CARED that Kitty owned the best and most comfortable piece of real estate on the ranch. I had bigger fish to fly.

Wait, hold everything. Did you notice that the subject of FISH popped up again? Could this be a clue? Had Pete infected our systems with some kind of Fish Virus? I mean, he's a dumb little cat but dumb in a cunning sort of way. You never want to estimunderate his talent for messing with the mind of a dog.

Maybe it was just a coincidence. Forget about the fish.

Okay, where were we? Oh yes, fish. Fish are pretty interesting little creatures and one of the great unanswered questions in this life is, "Who taught them to swim?" The same question applies to ducks. How is it that a duck can swim but if a buzzard falls into a stock tank, he'll sink like a rock?

An even better question is, why are we talking about fish, ducks, and buzzards? You see what Drover does to me? Phooey.

The point is that the lovely Sardina Bandana was sitting in the back of a pickup, not more than a hundred feet from the spot where our invasion force had come to a halt, and suddenly new meaning and purpose rushed into my life. My eyes grew wide with wonder and missification, and all at once my heart was beating like a beating heart.

"Sardina, my beloved, you've come back to me, just as I dreamed you would!"

Leaving Drover in charge of the troops, I went

rushing down the hill to see my darling, only I took a small detour that led to the yard fence. There, I glared through the wire and raised my voice to a thunder of righteous anger. "Pete, I have only one thing to say to you."

The pestilence lifted his head to a haughty angle and fluttered his eyelids. "Oh goodie, you're back. It's so boring when you're gone."

"Yeah? Well, try this on for size. I hope you get bedsores in your iris patch."

"Ooo, that was clever."

"And furthermore, take this!" Right there, in plain sight for all the world to see, *I stuck out my tongue at him . . . and even crossed my eyes!*

Boy, you talk about blowing a cat away! I blew him into next week, left him sputtering and speechless. The dumb cat. He thought I was lusting for his loafing spot in the shade? Ha, what a joke. I had much bigger and better things waiting for me—a gorgeous lady dog who absolutely adored me and a new assignment as Assistant Director of Bone Research at a very important arkinsawlogical excavation.

With all of this in my future, did I have time to fuss and twitter with the local cat? No sir. Poor old Pete. He had slid into insignificance, completely off the radar screen of my ambitions. Not

only would the Elite Troops of the Security Division not invade his yard, we wouldn't even give him a thought.

And so it was that I left the little sneak sitting in the ramble of his own rubble and marched around to the front of the house, where a vehicle was waiting to whisk me off to my new assignment. It would be a tough job, supervising a crew of scientists, and I'll admit that I felt a little nervous about it. I mean, I knew bones as well as any dog alive, but that other stuff—flint, beads, arrowheads, potterage—that wasn't exactly my cup of wax.

I would have to study and observe, and, well, bluff like crazy the rest of the time. You'd be surprised how well that works, bluffing. Heh heh.

I made my way toward the small crowd that had gathered at the front gate, where Mr. Wilkens, Little Alfred, and Sally May were engaged in conversation. Baby Molly was there too, but she was goo-gooing in her mother's arms and not actually a part of the conversation.

I slowed my pace to a dignified walk and shot a glance toward the pickup. Just as I suspected, the astonishingly beautiful Sardina Bandana was watching my every move, staring at me with eyes that sparkled like a whole trainload of diamonds.

To reward her attention, I raised one eyebrow, then hurried on to hear what was being said.

Sally May was talking. "Slim Chance? Why yes, he lives not far from here. In fact, he works for us on the ranch. How do you know Slim?"

"Well, we went to the same high school, and Slim and I . . ." Mr. Wilkens laughed and ducked his head. "We spent quite a lot of time together in the detention hall, catching up on our homework."

Sally May nodded. "That sounds like Slim. I'm sure a lot of teachers retired after he went through the school."

"We were both pretty caught up in being bronc riders, see, and couldn't seem to fit schoolwork into our schedules."

"But now you're an archeologist. What happened to the rodeo?"

"Well, ma'am, one night a bronc threw me so high, I caught a glimpse of the future. Riding to the hospital in the back of a 'fifty-seven Chevy pickup, I said to myself, 'Wilkie, the next pony is liable to break your neck. Maybe you ought to think about college.' I'd always been interested in archeology and here I am. I'm a contract archeologist, and I've been hired to do this excavation at the county park."

Little Alfred had been restless through this

conversation, and now he couldn't wait any longer. He tugged on his mother's dress. "Mom? Can I go?"

Sally May gave him a hard look. "Camp out on the hard ground? Sleep in a tent?" She turned to Mr. Wilkens. "Wouldn't he be in the way?"

"Not at all. We'll teach him to use a trowel and give him a little unit all to himself. By the time he leaves, he'll know a lot about archeology."

Alfred clasped his hands in the begging position. "Mom, please? I want to dig up a dinosaur."

Mr. Wilkens got a chuckle out of that. "Son, I'm afraid you won't find any dinosaurs on this dig. Our site isn't nearly that old. We think it's going to date somewhere around 1300 A.D. But it's an interesting site with a stone-enclosed house." He turned to Sally May. "What do you think?"

Sally May pondered. "It sounds like a wonderful opportunity. I'll discuss it with my husband when he comes back for lunch."

"Good. Well, I'd better get back to the dig. Alfred, thanks for the lemonade, and I'll hope to see you this afternoon."

As the pickup pulled away from the house, I caught a glimpse of Sardina Bandana. I'm almost sure that tears were flowing down her cheeks.

The poor dear! She was leaving without me and now she was crushed.

And come to think about it, I wasn't feeling so chirpy either. I had thought that I would be launching myself into a new career as a Digger of Ancient Bones, but now . . .

I didn't have time to think about the future, because Drover arrived at that very moment. He greeted me with his usual foolish grin. "Gosh, what happened?"

"Never mind what happened. I told you to stay with the troops."

"Yeah, but I couldn't find any."

"That's no excuse. You disobeyed an order, and it will go into my report."

"Oh drat. You look kind of disappointed."

"Oh? Well, maybe I am. To put it in a nutshell, my career has suddenly hit a snag."

"That's a funny way to put it."

"What's funny about snags?"

"No, I mean 'in a nutshell.' How come everybody puts things into nutshells?"

I stared into the vacuum of his eyes. "Drover, how do you come up with these questions?"

"Well, just think about it. Who has nutshells to put things into?" His eyes drifted up to the clouds. "Wouldn't it be easier to put things into baskets or dishpans?"

"It would be easier, but not as poetic. A nutshell captures the idea of smallness."

"Yeah, but what about coconuts?"

"What about them? They grow on trees and monkeys throw them at each other."

"Yeah, but they're not small."

"Well, that's your opinion. The fact is that all coconuts are not the same size. We have big ones and small ones, and the small ones are smaller than the big ones."

"Yeah, but you never hear about monkeys putting things into nutshells."

I stuck my nose into his face. "Drover, please don't try to draw me into a pointless argument. I don't care about monkeys."

"Well, you're the one who brought up nutshells."

"I'm sorry I brought it up. The point I was trying to put into a nutshell was that my career has suffered a blow. Furthermore, a charming, wonderful lady dog just left this ranch in tears."

"How can a ranch be left in tears?"

I felt my eyes bulging out. "The ranch was not in tears. Sardina Bandana was in tears when she left the ranch."

"Yeah, but she wasn't in tears."

"Of course she was. She had to leave without me."

"Well, when I saw her, she looked as happy as a lark."

I stared at the runt. "She *wasn't* as happy as a lark. She was merely trying to bear her sadness with dignity."

"I wonder if bears eat coconuts."

"What?"

"They walk kind of like monkeys."

"Drover, what are you babbling about? Monkeys, bears, coconuts . . . none of it makes any sense!"

He shook his head. "I know. All I did was ask about nutshells."

"Nutshells? I'll show you nutshells. YOU'RE a nutshell! Good-bye, and please don't ever speak to me again."

I hurried away from the little goof, never suspecting that I would . . . well, you'll see, but I'll give you a little hint. I got involved in a big real estate deal and rented myself . . . *an air-conditioned office!*

CHAPTER TEN

I Do Business
with the Cat

Pretty exciting, huh? You bet, and here's how it happened.

After enduring that loopy conversation with Drover about nutshells and monkeys, I hurried away before he could draw me any deeper into the swamp of his mind. I mean, Drover is a nice little guy in some ways, but carrying on a normal conversation with him can be very discouraging. He talks in circles and spirals, and before you know it . . . never mind.

The point is that I had escaped with most of my mind intact. I hurried down the yard fence and happened to catch a glimpse at Mister Kitty Perfect, lounging in cool air-conditioned comfort of his iris patch. As I blew past, he perked up and waved.

Did I speak or wave back? Absolutely not. Speaking to cats is not only a tee-total waste of time, it's also against regulations. No sir, I blew past him and made my way up the hill to the . . . boy, it was hot!

I slowed my trudge up the hill. I stopped. I turned my gaze back to the cool greenness of Sally May's yard and . . . uh, found myself easing back down the hill and to the yard fence.

I threw glances over both shoulders, just to be sure that Drover wasn't around to spy on me. He wasn't. I had no idea where he went and I didn't care. At least he was out of my life for a while.

I, uh, drifted down the fence and . . . well, noticed Pete on the other side, sitting in the shade. You know, it never hurts to be neighborly to the neighbors, even if one of your neighbors happens to be a cat. I know, I know, we have rules against flatternizing with kitties, but speaking to them every once in a while doesn't cause any great harm.

"Hey, Pete, how's it going?"

He smirked and waved a paw. "Hello, Hankie. You're back."

"Ha ha. I wouldn't put it exactly that way, Pete. I mean, to say 'You're back' makes it sound as though, well, you've been expecting me."

"Um-hm. I have been. What can I do for you, Hankie?"

"Oh, nothing. No, I was just, you know, out on a stroll and saw you there and thought I'd be neighborly and say howdy. No kidding."

"Howdy. It's hot out there in the sun, isn't it?"

"Oh, it's not so bad. No, I kind of like the heat." I gazed up at the flaming ball of sun overhead and felt myself melting. I leaned toward the cat and lowered my voice. "Okay, Pete, what would it take to rent your iris patch?"

He took a moment to buff his claws on his chest. "Three days' scraps for one day's rent."

"Pete, that's outrageous!" The cat shrugged. I ran his numbers through my spreadsheet application. "Okay, maybe we can work with your numbers, but there's one problem. Sally May."

He gave me a wink. "She's through watering the flowers and she won't come outside again today. I know her habits. She'll never suspect a thing."

I began pacing back and forth, as I often do when my mind is reaching into new and unexplored territory. I submitted kitty's deal to another blistering analysis, checked every detail and number, did the math forward and backward.

I marched back to the cat. "Okay, Pete, we've

got ourselves a deal." All at once the cat started . . . I don't know what. Coughing or sneezing or choking. "What's the problem?"

"Oh, nothing. Just a little . . . hee hee . . . sneezing spell."

"It's probably all this dust. So when do I take possession?"

"Well, Hankie, we might as well get started now, huh?"

Pete was still struggling with his allergy attack, but he managed to climb outside the fence and I leaped over into the yard. I looked at him through the fence.

"This is something new, isn't it? Me in the yard and you outside in the heat and the dust. How times change! I mean, who would have ever thought the day would come when you and I would do business together?"

He stared at me for a long moment with his weird yellow eyes. "Well, Hankie, none of my nasty tricks work any more. Maybe I'll think of some new ones."

I chuckled. "You can always hope, kitty."

"And maybe, after you've spent some time in the shade, you'll . . . get careless."

That got a big laugh. "Ha ha ha. Don't count on it, Pete. See, you're dealing with the Head of

Ranch Security, not some ordinary mutt like Drover. The Head of Ranch Security never gets careless."

"We'll see, I guess."

"You bet. Oh, say, here's a thought. Since we've just cut a major business deal, maybe we ought to shake on it."

"Maybe we should, Hankie."

He came toward the fence and stuck his entire front leg through the fence wire. Instead of giving his paw a shake—hee hee, you'll love this part—I stood on it, so that he couldn't move. Hee hee.

He shot me a daggerish glare and began twitching the last two inches of his tail. "Hankie, this isn't polite."

"Yeah? Well, get used to it, kitty. Oh, by the way, I would have paid twice the rent you're charging. Ha ha! Enjoy the heat."

And with that, I marched away from the little sneak, left him crushed and broken, and took possession of my new air-conditioned office in the iris patch.

What a deal!

Boy, you talk about a great place to be in the heat of summer! Wow. Five minutes after I'd moved into the iris patch, I knew that it was not only the best, coolest, refreshingest spot on the ranch, but maybe even in the whole world.

It was on the shady side of the house, see, and the ground stayed damp because it was out of the sun. But even better was the fact that a cool breeze swept around the corner of the house, a great little breeze.

Yes sir, the iris patch and I were going to get along fine. Why, if I'd known it was such a pleasant spot, I would have evicted the cat long ago. Come to think of it, why hadn't I? Oh yes. Sally May. But we had solved the Sally May problem, hadn't we?

Pretty shrewd, huh? See, I had figured out that once she'd done her daily watering, she would stay in the house for the rest of the day. Okay, maybe Pete had pointed this out, but the fact remained that she would stay in the house during the heat of the day. And I had figured it out on my own.

Had I made a great deal or what? Heh heh. What a dumbbell! Kitty Kitty was out in the heat and I was in the shade, and for that I had given up *three measly days of scraps*! See, what Pete didn't know—and what you haven't known up to this very moment—is that on miserable hot days, I don't care about scraps anyway.

But there's more still. I had every reason to

suspect that after Poor Kitty spent the rest of the day baking in the sun, he would lose his appetite too, and when scrap time came around, he would discover the awful truth about our deal.

He had traded his air-conditioned iris patch for something worthless!

Ha ha, ho ho, hee hee.

I loved it! I'm sorry, I don't mean to gloat about this, but you have to remember that Pete and I had a long and bitter history. The little snot had pulled many cheap tricks on me and had gotten me in trouble more times than I could count. Now that I had skinned him in a business deal, I just . . . well, I couldn't hold back my devilish joy and delight.

It was turning into one of the finest days of my career.

Yes sir, there I was in the World's Coolest . . . the only problem with the iris patch was . . . well, the irises. The iris plants made a lumpy bed, shall we say, and after I'd occupied the spot for thirty minutes or so, I decided to, uh, rearrange the furniture. We needed to move the sofa over here and the chair over there and soften up the bed a little bit.

This required some . . . well, digging, you might say. Not much. I mean, I sure didn't want to make any drastic changes to the, uh, decorum because, well, Sally May might not approve.

Sally May *wouldn't* approve, no question about it. No, these were just little changes, tiny rearrangements of the, uh, facilities.

Dig dig. Hack hack. Scrape scrape.

Have you ever tried to rearrange a patch of irises? It's not as easy as you might think. In the first place, irises grow in clumps and they're tough little plants. In the second place, when you lie on top of them, they poke you in many awkward places, such as the rib cage and belly.

That's exactly why the people who build mattresses have never made a mattress stuffed with iris plants. They would go broke trying to sell an iris mattress to the American public.

Scrape scrape, hack hack.

But I'm no quitter. To quote the words of Slim Chance, "If at first you don't succeed, get a bigger hammer." It took a while to get those stubborn irises arranged just right, but I got 'er done. And then . . .

WOW!

Cool breeze, cool ground, cool air, cool shade . . . all of that amidst the fragrance of fresh iris juice! And let me tell you, fellers, fresh iris juice smells pretty nice.

I didn't think my life could get any better, but you know what? It got better. As I was lying there, letting the cool breeze tickle my ears, I began to notice Pete. Remember him? The dumbbell, the guy I had recently trounced in a big real estate deal?

Hee hee, ha ha, ho ho. Sorry, but this part is so funny, I can hardly control myself.

He'd been out in the heat for an hour, see, and it was starting to grind him down. You know what he did? He started whining and moaning! Yes sir, whining and moaning and yowling about all the misery his pampered little body was finding out there in the Real World.

Did I feel sorry for him? Heh heh. You've probably guessed.

No, I didn't feel sorry for him. I ate it up, gobbled it down in huge bites and savored every morsel of his unhappiness. You know why? *Because he deserved it.* I'd spent years hoping to cause the little creep this kind of misery, and now, all of a sudden, I had him just where he wanted me.

Get this. After whimpering at the yard gate for an hour, he made his way around the fence and took up a position only ten feet away from my new office. And there, he set up a pitiful moan-

and-cry routine that was calculated to . . . I don't know what. Make me feel some sympathy, I suppose.

Moaning and yowling, he said, "Oh, Hankie, I never realized just how hot and miserable it could be out here!"

"No kidding? Well, education is always expensive. Now you know what I've been living with all these years."

"But Hankie, I'm not as big and tough as you."

"Pete, that's the price you pay for being a sniveling little cat. Stop complaining."

"But Hankie, I'm beginning to feel that I made a bad trade."

I snorted with laughter. "Go easy, Pete, you're about to break my heart."

"Won't you reconsider and let me have my iris patch back?"

"Look, pal, we made a deal, fair and square. The fact that it was a bonehead deal is what we call 'too bad.'"

"But Hankie, I'm so hot and miserable!"

I was loving this. "Look at the brighter side, kitty. Your misery is bringing joy to others. After all these years of being a selfish little creep, you're finally making the world a brighter place. Oh, and I'd appreciate it if you'd tone down the moaning. I'm fixing to take a nap and I'd rather not listen to your noise."

He stared at me with wide eyes. "You mean . . . you mean you could sleep while I'm in such misery?"

"Yes. Like a log. Like a chunk of petrified wood. Good night."

I lowered my enormous body down into the cool embrace of the shaded ground and . . . wow, you talk about a great place for a nap! It couldn't have been better.

Well, it might have been better if Pete had shut up his noise, but you know what? Certain dogs have the ablurtity to shut all snorks out of their murks, and they can actually porkchop the honking sasafrass and snurp through all kinds of noizzzzzzzzzzzzzzzzzzzzz . . . .

Through the haze of delicious sleep, I heard a woman's voice say, "Pete? Kitty kitty? What's wrong? Where are you? Oh, there you are, but what . . . HANK! What are you . . . *look what you've done to my flower bed, you hound!*"

HUH?

My eyes popped open.

Sally May? She was standing over me with . . . uh-oh . . . with flared nostrils and flaming eyeballs.

A Thermonuclear
Moment

I blinked my eyes and glanced around at my . . . uh . . . surroundings. Gulp. I was in her yard, it seemed, and even lying in her . . . yipes . . . in her former iris patch, which I had . . .

But wait, she wasn't supposed to come back outside in the heat of the day, remember? Pete and I had already decided . . .

It was then that I caught a glimpse of the cat. He was sitting on the other side of the fence, grinning at me and waving his paw. And then he said—this is an exact quote, you might want to write it down—he said in his whiny, simpering voice, "Guess what, Hankie. I learned a new trick."

HUH?

Suddenly all the pieces of the puzzle began . . .

oh boy, I had really stepped into a bear trap this time. Was there any chance that I could talk my way out of it? Was there any hope that I could salvage what was left of my relationship with Sally May?

She towered over me, her fists resting on her hips. You know that dangerous wrinkle-line that sometimes appears in the middle of her forehead? It was there, and she sure looked . . . well, mad. Furious. Uncommonly angry.

Gulp.

In a flash, I switched all systems over to the special emergency message we call "I Can Explain Everything, No Kidding." My tail began tapping out a slow rhythm of Deepest Remorse. I dropped my ears into the Pitiful Position and beamed her a look that was heavy with sadness and regret, a look that said:

"Sally May, I know what you're thinking and . . . okay, I'll admit that it looks pretty bad, but hear me out. You see, it was hot and I just couldn't resist . . . the irises were poking me in the ribs, see, and I had to . . . but the bottom line, Sally May, is that your cat set up this whole deal and I was just an innocent . . ."

It wasn't working, I could see it in her eyes, in her face, in her clenched fists. She sucked in a deep breath of air and thundered, "Where's my broom!" And she stomped around the corner of the house.

Broom? Hey, I knew about her broom. I had met her broom several times before, and it had never been what you'd call a pleasant experience. It was time to, uh, scuttle the ship, shall we say.

Fellers, I was in big trouble.

I would be the last dog in the world to say a harsh word about my master's wife, and yet . . . and yet there are times when she doesn't seem to be . . . well, totally rational.

I mean, we've already discussed the heat, the terrible heat, and she should have understood that when a dog lives out in the heat, day after boiling day, he begins to crave greenness and softness and shadeness. And when he looks across the fence and sees . . .

Well, she didn't understand, and I knew it the very moment she mentioned the broom. "Broom" is a four-letter word which means that the path of reason has been abandoned. It means that at least one of the parties in the dispute is angry. And, finally, it means that . . . well, the other party in the dispute had better run for cover.

A five-letter word. "Broom" has five letters, not four.

When Sally May disappeared around the corner of the house, I began preparing my Broom Countermeasures Program. It appeared that the best course of action would be to make a dash for the nearest fence, dive over the top, and head for Tallest Timber, as we say. Yes, that was an excellent plan. It would not only allow me to save my life, but it would also prevent Sally May from wrapping that broom around my ears.

I was about to Launch All Dogs, when my ears picked up the sounds of someone . . . laughing. Giggling. Guffawing. I swung my gaze around toward the sound and saw . . . you'll never guess who or whom or what I saw.

Or maybe you would. It was Pete, and okay, maybe that was pretty obvious, but the impointant point is that the sounds of his laughter disrupted my Launch Program. All at once I forgot about Sally May and the broom, and lumbered over to the fence and confronted the cat.

"I guess you think you're pretty clever, Pete."

"Well, Hankie, the facts pretty muchly speak for themselves."

"Don't try to deny it, kitty. Your fingerprints are all over this deal. I tried to do business with you, and what did you do? You went behind my back, schemed and weaseled, and lured me into a trap."

He batted his eyelids and grinned. "I did, Hankie, and you know what? It was so easy, I almost feel guilty. You didn't just take the bait; you ate the whole can of worms!" He broke into a fit of laughter.

I glared at him through the fence, and a deep rumbling growl began working its way up from the dark depths of my inner bean. "Go ahead, Pete, laugh it up, enjoy yourself. But there's one little detail you forgot. Once I leave the yard, you'll . . ."

WHACK!

Huh? Oh yes, the broom, and maybe it had been foolish of me to, uh, postpone the Launch All Dogs Procedure, because . . .

WHACK!

. . . because there was a crazy woman in the yard. She was armed with a deadly broom and . . .

WHACK!

"Get out of my yard, you oaf! Hike! Scat!"

. . . and if I didn't do something fast, she was liable to do great harm to my . . .

WHACK!

I ran, fellers. The Launch Program fell by the hayseed and I went sprinting around the side of the house. Would you believe that *she followed me,* came after me with that deadly broom poised over her head? She did.

I could hardly believe it—a grown woman, a mother of two children, a productive member of society, chasing her loyal dog around the house! In daily broadlight.

WHACK!

She missed on that one, but not by much. Was there any chance we could call a truce and, well, patch things up?

WHACK!

No. It appeared that we had moved beyond patching things up.

"Get out of my yard, and don't come back!"

Okay, fine. She wanted me out of her yard, so I altered course and headed straight for the . . .

BONK!

. . . fence, only at the last second I forgot to, uh, engage the landing gear, shall we say. Okay, I forgot to jump and ran into the fence. The collision set off a spray of checkers and colored lights behind my eyes, but this was the wrong time to pause and enjoy the fireworks display. I regained my feet and sprinted around the south side of the house.

At that very moment, Little Alfred came outside to see what was going on. When he saw the situation, he chirped a little laugh and said,

"Hey, Mom, what are you doing? Are you chasing Hank with the bwoom?"

To which she screeched, "Your father's dog destroyed, and I mean *destroyed,* my iris patch, and if I ever get my hands on him . . ."

Alfred's eyes grew wide, and I was disappointed, very disappointed, to see his smile increase in size. "Uh-oh, Hankie, you'd better run!"

Yes, I was aware of that, and in fact I *was* running. The problem, he might have noticed, was that his mother—again, a mature woman and a mother of two children—was also running and seemed very serious about . . .

Somehow, in the midst of all the excitement and so forth, none of us had noticed that a car had pulled up in front of the house, or that two ladies had gotten out and were standing at the front gate. I noticed them when I came zooming around the northeast corner of the house.

They were strangers. I had never seen them before. I paused just a moment to . . .

WHACK!

Down came the broom (it missed me by an inch), and that's when Sally May saw the ladies. She stopped in her tracks. An awful silence moved over us. The ladies stared at Sally May, as though . . . well, let's face it, as though they were watching something really bizarre. And they were.

Sally May's eyes flicked back and forth. Her face turned pink and then red, as she realized . . . she was dressed in ragged cutoff jeans and an old shirt, her hair looked like a buzzard's nest, she was chasing her loyal dog around the yard . . . and she had visitors.

Her eyes rolled up inside her head, and I heard her mumble, "I can't believe this." Neither could I, but I took this opportunity to dive into a cedar shrub in front of the house and wiggle myself into the safety of its depths. There, I peered through the underbrush and watched.

The ladies exchanged worried glances, then one of them said, "Maybe we came at a bad time."

Sally May gave them a crazy smile. "Oh no, it's just another day in paradise. We live like this all the time. Can I help you with something?"

"We're with the Census Bureau."

Sally May pushed a sprig of hair out of her eyes. "The Census Bureau. Oh good."

"Honey, I know you've already sent in your form—and we thank you for that—but we had a few more questions to ask." The lady frowned at some papers in her hand. "How many toilets do you have in your house?"

Sally May's eyes settled on the woman. "Toilets? Two."

"And sinks or washbasins?"

"Two."

"Is that counting the kitchen sink?"

"No."

"So . . . you have a total of three sinks and washbasins?" Sally May said nothing. The woman wrote down the information. "Has anyone in your family ever suffered from a mental disorder?"

Sally May's eyes were glittering with a kind of strange light. "Why yes. I suffered one five minutes ago when I found that my husband's dog had dug up my flower bed. I was hoping to strangle him when you drove up."

The ladies traded glances. "Maybe . . . maybe we should come back another time."

"I think that's a wonderful idea. I don't mean to be rude, but I'm not having a good day."

The ladies smiled and said good-bye, hurried back to their car, and drove away. Just then, Little Alfred came around the side of the house.

"Who was that, Mom?"

Sally May buried her face in her hands. "It was the Census Bureau, for crying out loud, the United States government! They're gathering information about how we live . . . and they saw me . . ." She let out a moan, then uncovered her face. All at once her eyes seemed . . . well, on fire, and she hissed, *"Where is that dog!"*

Uh-oh.

I didn't dare breathe or move a muscle. In the eerie silence, I heard her footsteps in the yard. They were coming closer to the shrubberies in which I was hiding and cringing.

I heard her voice. "Hank! Get out of my yard!"

Did she really think I was going to expose myself to her broom? Ha. We could forget that. Was it my fault that the census ladies had shown up just as she was chasing me around the house? No, but you'll notice that I got blamed for it.

All at once she started slapping the shrub with her broom. Whap, whap, whap!

"Hank, if I get my hands on you, so help me I'll . . ."

I guess she didn't know that there was a big yellowjacket wasp nest in the bush or that her broom-whamming would get them stirred up.

Even more important was the fact that I didn't know it either, so I can't be held responsible. I was just an innocent bystander, a faithful dog who was trying to figure out how to please the people in his life.

Anyway, she managed to get the wasps really

stirred up. When she saw the yellowjackets pouring out of the bush, she let out a screech, dropped her broom, gathered up Little Alfred, and they both dived inside the house, one step ahead of the entire Yellowjacket Air Force.

You'll be disappointed to know that her last words, as she scrambled inside the house, were, and this is a direct quote: "If I ever see that dog again . . . !"

The Cremated
Roast Beef

W ords can't express how deeply those words cut into the crick of my quick. They hurt me terribly. I mean, the very idea that my master's wife would blame *me* for the Wasp Incident . . . I had tried so hard to work out a peaceful solution to our . . .

Oh well. Life is often cruel and unfair. We dogs get blamed for crimes we didn't commit, and we're forced to take it. That's just part of our job.

The important thing is that I had survived Sally May's latest Thermonuclear Moment, but before I could make a run for safety, I heard the sound of an approaching vehicle. Was it possible that the census ladies had returned to ask more questions about toilets and sinks? If so, they didn't know Sally May as well as I knew her.

I peered out of the shrubberies and saw the ranch's flatbed pickup approaching. It pulled up in front of the house. The doors opened and out stepped Loper and Slim. As they walked toward the house, I heard them talking.

Slim: "Well, the windmill's fixed and pumping water, so maybe you can force up a cheerful attitude."

Loper: "We got lucky. It'll probably break down again this afternoon."

Slim: "It ain't going to break down, 'cause it was repaired by a couple of windmill geniuses."

Loper: Even if the mill pumps day and night, the tank won't fill up for three days."

Slim: "So we'll haul water. That's what that water trailer's for."

Loper: "It'll take six loads. We'll be hauling water until midnight."

Slim: "Well, so what? I know you ain't got any social engagements, 'cause nobody but me could stand to be around you for more than five minutes . . . and I'm starting to have second thoughts myself."

Loper: "Very funny. I hope Sally May's got a big lunch ready. I'm starved."

They moseyed up the sidewalk and stepped

up on the front porch. There, they pulled off their dirty boots with the boot jack. (That was another of Sally May's Rules: no dirty boots in the house.) They removed their boots and socks, and Loper began swatting at the swarm of wasps that had lingered on the porch.

"Dadgum yellowjackets! Boy, they sure get bad this time of year."

At that very moment, the door opened and Sally May stepped outside. From my hiding place in the shrubberies, I scanned her face to determine . . . oops, she still looked mad.

Loper greeted her with a smile. "There's Mrs. America! Hi, hon, we're starved."

"I've just cremated the roast."

Slim and Loper traded glances. Loper said, "I've always liked my beef well-done, how about you, Slim?"

"Oh yeah, you bet."

Sally May's eyes flashed. "It's not well-done, it's cremated! Blackened! Scorched! Charred! And do you know why?"

She told them the story of her morning, which included . . . would you like to guess who got blamed for cremating the roast beef? ME.

I mean, had I put the roast into the oven? Had I turned on the fire? Had I devoted my whole

morning to ruining her lunch plans? No sir, but that didn't matter. I got blamed for it anyway.

Okay, maybe the Incident in the Iris Patch had played a small role in the overall situation, but let me hasten to add . . . oh well.

Sally May told them about the census ladies. "There I was, chasing *your dog* around the yard, looking like Wild Mag, the trapper's wife, and those women saw the whole thing. I've never been so humiliated! I could have died!"

Slim and Loper tried to bite back their smiles, but they couldn't help laughing. They roared. Sally May glared at them, and for a long moment it appeared that she might erupt into another Thermonuclear Moment, but then she smiled, and even laughed.

"I guess it is kind of funny, now that it's over. I hope you're still laughing after you eat that roast."

"We'll love it, hon. Don't worry about a thing. Let's eat."

Sally May lifted a finger in the air. "Not yet." She told the men about her conversation with Mr. Wilkens. She turned to Slim. "He said you two were friends."

Slim slouched against one of the porch posts. "He admitted it, huh? That was brave of him.

Yep, we rode a few broncs together. Wilkie retired one night in Guymon when a big bald-faced horse stepped on his hat."

Sally May frowned. "Stepped on his hat?"

"Yeah, his head was in it. It must have jarred something loose, 'cause when he got out of the hospital, he enrolled in college."

Sally May said, "Oh," and turned back to Loper. "Well, he's invited Alfred to camp out with them and take part in the excavation."

Loper nodded. "Good, good. Great opportunity to learn about archeology."

"I'd feel more comfortable if *you* went with him. He's only five years old."

Loper's eyes bugged out. "Me? Hon, they do archeology with dentist tools! That would drive me nuts. Scrape, scrape. Pick, pick." Sally May waited. Slim smirked. "And besides, we're out of water in the middle pasture. Those cows are standing on their heads to get a drink. We'll be hauling water all day and into the night."

Sally May fiddled with a button on her blouse. "How many cowboys does it take to haul water?"

Slim nodded. "You know, I hadn't thought of that. Loper, I can haul that water and you can go learn all about archeology. I'll bet you'd really enjoy it."

Loper's eyes darted back and forth. "Let me think about it. We might have to reschedule some of our work."

Sally May stepped toward the door. "Alfred would be disappointed if he couldn't go. Oh, and your dog is hiding in the bushes. Would you mind showing him the gate? Thanks."

She went into the house, leaving the two men and a heavy silence. Loper turned to Slim. "So you're all excited about hauling water, huh?"

"Well, I wouldn't say excited, but I'm always glad to volunteer my service to the ranch."

"No kidding?"

"Well, sure." Slim hitched up his jeans. "I mean, how many times does a grumpy rancher get invited to dig around in the dirt with a toothpick . . . in the heat of summer?" Slim snorted a laugh. "I'm sure it'll raise your IQ a couple of points, and everybody knows you need some help."

"You're enjoying this, aren't you?"

"Uh-huh. I just wish I could be there with a camera. Heh."

Loper rocked up and down on his toes and gazed off in the distance. "You know, Slim, one of the most satisfying parts of being the boss on an outfit like this is . . . you can grant wishes."

Slim stared at him, and I noticed that the corners of his mouth began to sag. "What are you talking about?"

"Wishes. You wished that you could be there with a camera, so we'll borrow Sally May's camera."

"Wait a second, hold on. Loper, I hope you ain't thinking . . ."

Loper draped his arm over Slim's shoulder. "You know, Slimbo, this water situation is so serious, I think we'd better let top management handle it. I'm sure you'll agree."

Slim brushed his arm away. "I'm sure I *don't* agree."

"You'll get to spend some time with your old friend."

"He ain't as good a friend as I thought. And if it makes any difference, I've never had the slightest interest in archeology."

Loper gave that some serious thought. "Slim, one part of me feels your pain. The other part of me just doesn't care. Pack your toothbrush, buddy."

"You've got to be kidding me!"

"No. And come to think of it, you better pack a couple of toothbrushes. You might be digging with one of them." Loper let out a wicked cackle.

"See you inside. And throw Bozo out of the yard, would you?"

Loper went inside and the door closed behind him. Slim glared at the door for a moment, then raised a bony fist into the air and yelled, "One of these days, the hired hands of this world are going to rise up and revolt! It ain't fair! And, Loper, you're a low-down skunk!"

Slim stood there, scowling, then stepped off the porch in his bare feet and came creeping over to the shrubbery in which I was . . . well, hiding. I stopped breathing and didn't move a muscle. Maybe he wouldn't see me. Maybe he'd think . . .

Suddenly I saw his face through the bushes, and heard his voice. "Hi, puppy. I see you."

Yes, well, I saw him too, but if he thought . . . I switched the tail section over to Slow Taps.

"Hank, I'd be mighty proud if you'd get out of Sally May's yard."

Right, I understood his wishes, but the fact of the matter was that . . . well, cedar shrubs make shade, and I had sort of decided . . . that is, if it was okay with him, I might just stay in the shade of the shrubberies.

He dropped his smile. His face turned into a mask of angry lines and fangs and bulging eyeballs, and suddenly he began screeching at me.

"Get out of the yard, or I'll kick your tail up between your ears! Get out!"

Okay, fine. Hey, if I'd known he was so serious about it . . . he didn't need to screech at me. Dogs have feelings, too.

When he started yelling and shaking the shrub, I decided that . . . well, maybe he wanted me to leave the yard, right? And maybe he was pretty serious about it, and it appeared that our attempts to negotiate a settlement had, uh, ended in failure.

I ran toward daylight, exploded out of the shrubberies, squirted between his legs, sprinted across the yard, and flew over the fence as gracefully as a deer. Behind me, I heard a scream of pain.

"Eeeee-yowwww!"

Okay, Slim had found the wasp nest, or they had found him, and one or more of the little monsters had nailed him with their stingers. Well, that was too bad. I refused to take responsibility for his wasp stings, and Slim got exactly what he deserved for being such a rude person.

Once I left the green pastures of Sally May's yard, I found myself in the heartless grisp of Endless July. I began to wilt and melt. All the bodily rhythms of my body began to slow and sink. I started panting. Precious drops of water dripped off my tongue, and all at once I felt myself being pulled into the Black Hole of Molasses.

I slowed from a run to a walk, then flopped down in some pitiful fried weeds that gave no more shade than . . . something. Than a bunch of pitiful fried weeds. And there my body shut down all but the most vital of functions. And I sang a song to protest the dreadful heat. Here's how it went.

I'm Burning Up!

I'm burning up, I am boiling.
A dog can hardly function when he's broiling.
This coat of hair is hotter than a furnace top.
I really really wish that I could take it off.

The elements are conspiring to corrode my
    will.
My job and everything I do have lost their
    thrill.
If a blizzard were to come, it would sure be
    nice.
I would give a pretty penny for a piece of ice.

I'm being barbecued alive on the grill of fate.
Sizzling and popping on the sun's hot grate.
I tried to fool myself to think I just don't care,
Then realized my temperature was medium
    rare.

Let me ask you, how's a dog supposed to
    function in this heat?
I have a job and many duties that I must
    complete.
I am trying to convince myself that the
    weather's nice and cool,
But here I am, a guinea pig in someone's
    cooking school!

I am dying in this heat, I'm being scorched
    alive.
I don't know if it's better to be stewed or
    fried.
My juices have been boiled and there's
    nothing left.
The thing that really puzzles me is . . . who's
    the chef?

So there you are. That's the kind of song a dog
sings when he's being boiled and fried in the sun.

CHAPTER THIRTEEN

I Get Demoted

At 1:00 or thereabouts, Slim and Loper came out of the house and walked to the yard gate. There, they stopped. Loper glanced over both shoulders and said, "She was right. That roast was cremated."

"Well, it was better than boiled owl."

They shared a laugh, then Loper yawned and stretched his arms. "I'm going to hook up the trailer and start hauling water, but I want you to know that I'll be with you in spirit. Don't forget your bedroll. That ground gets hard in the middle of the night."

Slim gave him a scorching glare. "You ain't one bit funny, Loper, and there will be a time for paybacks."

"Have fun."

Loper headed for his pickup, whistling a tune. Slim's gaze followed him and he muttered, "A man invests a small fortune in cowboy gear, and they send him off to summer camp! Baloney."

Loper drove away in a cloud of dust, just as Alfred and his momma came out of the house. Alfred was loaded down with camping gear and his eyes were sparkling with excitement. The boy said, "I'm all ready, Swim. This is going to be fun!"

Slim ran a toothpick through his mouth and grumbled, "I'll bet."

Well, it appeared that the moment had arrived for Our Team to leave for the excavation site. In my spot in the wilted weeds, I launched myself into the Jack and Lift Procedure. In the terrible heat, this was no small matter.

First, I lifted the front half of my enormous body and propped it up on my two front legs. Next, I jacked up the hind end and slipped my two back legs beneath it. Then and only then did I test the entire structure to see if it would carry the full weight of my body. It did, and I made my way down the hill to the yard gate.

When Alfred saw me, he beamed a smile. "And Hankie can go with us!"

There was a moment of dead silence. Slim and

Sally May exchanged looks, and she said, "I don't think so."

"But Mom, Mr. Wilkens has *his* dog."

"Honey, his dog has manners. Your dog spent his whole morning trying to drive me batty. He doesn't deserve any privileges."

"But Mom . . ."

Slim nodded. "Your momma's right. One dog on an archeology site is probably enough."

Sally May leaned toward Slim and whispered, "When you leave, I'll lock him in the barn, so he won't follow you."

What?

Did you hear that? I couldn't believe my ears. Leave me behind? Deny me the opportunity to expand my career? There must be some mistake. I turned toward Slim and proceeded to give him Sad Eyes and Spiritually Wounded Tail. Maybe it would work. Don't forget that Slim and I had a long history of . . .

He didn't notice, didn't even look at me. Okay, we were down to Sally May and . . . gulp. You know, when you're down to Sally May, you're down to . . . not much. Over the years, I had tried SO HARD to live up to her expectations of Good Dogness, but somehow, when she and I occupied the same space for a few minutes, things went wrong.

Could I change her heart and mind? I had to give it a shot. I squeezed up a facial expression called "I Ask So Little" and hoped it might soften her heart.

"No."

Huh? Hey, I hadn't even gotten to the good part.

"No."

Would it help if I licked her on the ankle?

"Stop that!"

See? What did I tell you? Down in flames. Nothing works on that woman.

I cranked my tail up between my legs, lowered my head, and slunk away—shamed, disgraced, rejected by the very woman to whom I had devoted my life to. I switched my eyes over to a routine we call I'm Not Sure I'll Make It Through the Day and even provoked a spell of coughing. Sometimes that will touch the hearts of the women-folk, coughing.

From my deathbed, I watched them. They loaded the camping gear into Slim's pickup. Alfred gave his mother a hug. "Bye, Mom. I sure wish my dad could come with me."

"I know you do, sweetie, but he's worried about the cattle." She gave Slim a pat on the arm. "Slim, this is very kind of you, and I know Loper appreciates it."

"Yes, he mentioned that."

"It's just too bad this water situation came up."

"Yalp. Well, Button, let's load up. The excitement is starting to build."

They got into Slim's pickup, waved one last good-bye, and drove away. Only then did the cinder block of truth come crashing down upon my head. *They had actually left me behind!* I was trying to work my way through this crushing development when Drover arrived.

He glanced around. "I'll be derned. You're not going?"

"That's correct."

"Did you get in trouble with Sally May . . . again?"

"That's one way of putting it. Yes."

"Maybe you'd better stay out of her yard."

I gave him a withering glare. "Drover, when I need advice from you, I'll ask for it. Now, please hush. Oh, and hold my calls. I don't wish to be disturbed."

"Yeah, but Sally May just called your name."

"What?"

He pointed his paw. "She's calling you. Maybe she changed her mind."

I moved my gaze toward the yard gate and saw her standing there. She wore a friendly smile, and she was calling my name in a pleasant tone of voice. "Hank? Come here, boy."

I whirled back to Drover. "Excuse me, I've just received an important call. It appears that Sally May has begun to regret her cruel and shabby treatment of me and wants to make a complete apology."

"How sweet!"

I squared my shoulders and trotted down to the gate. Would I be gracious enough to accept her apology? Sure. Of course. To be honest, I couldn't understand why it had taken her so long to patch things up, but as they say, "Better late than later." By George, if she was willing to walk the first mile, I could sure walk the second step.

She had parked Baby Molly in the stroller and was standing beside the yard gate, beaming a warm smile in my direction. As I approached her, I found myself thinking, "Why couldn't it be this way all the time?" How had things gotten so badly out of kilter? It was a crying shame that two grown, mature individuals . . .

What was that thing in her hand? A long piece of leather? What was she doing with . . . HUH? I stopped in my tracks.

"Come on, boy, come here."

All of a sudden I remembered what she'd

whispered to Slim, something about "When you leave, I'll lock him in the barn." You'd forgotten about that, but I hadn't. No sir, and I had a pretty good idea who the "him" was. ME. And getting myself locked up in a dungeon wasn't going to fit into my schedule.

She sensed that something was afoot. Her smile slipped a couple of notches and her voice acquired an edge. "Hank, come here! Now."

I, uh, went to Slow Swings on the tail section and avoided her gaze. I had always taken pride in being a loyal, obedient dog, but she was putting me in an impossible situation. Could we discuss this? I mean, I had already made plans for the rest of the day and, well, I'd never been fond of leashes.

"Hank!"

She took a step in my direction and snapped her fingers. That was a bad sign. When Sally May goes to snapping those fingers, you'd better take cover. I began edging away.

Her eyes flared. "Hank, come here this minute!"

I hadn't planned to run, honest. I mean, running away from her could have been interpreted as a sign of disobedience, but when she lunged toward me with her hands shaped like claws, what was I supposed to do, sit there and say "Duh?"

No sir, I did what any normal, healthy American dog would have done. I did a quick one-eighty, pushed the throttle to Turbo Three, and headed for a better climate, so to speak.

"Hank, come back here! So help me, if I ever get my hands on you . . ."

Now, what kind of moron would stop after hearing *that*? Did I really want to find out what she would do if she ever got her hands on me? I had a pretty good idea—unscrew my neck, shake me until my eyeballs fell out, lock me in the deep freeze, something awful—and I found myself pushing the throttle up to Turbo Four.

Behind me, she screeched, "Disobedient hound!"

I felt pretty bad about the whole situation and knew it wasn't going to help our relationship, but gee whiz . . . if she had tried a softer approach, maybe we could have worked things out, but when she came after me with her claws . . . oh well. It was water under the brig.

I went streaking away from the house, past the machine shed, past the chicken house, and down the hill toward the corrals, setting a course to the west. Maybe you think I spent the rest of the day hiding out and trembling in fear that

Sally May might track me down and lock me up in the barn.

No sir. By the time I reached the west side of ranch headquarters, two things had happened. A New Plan for the Future had begun to glow in the back of my mind and Drover had caught up with me.

He arrived, huffing and puffing. "Boy, that was scary. What happened?"

"She was plotting to lock me up for the rest of the day."

"I'll be derned. Why would she do that?"

"'Cause she thought I might go running off to the lake."

"Aw heck, you'd never do that. Would you?"

I gave him a steely glare. "Of course I would. They need me over there, Drover, and a cowdog always goes where he's needed."

"Who's 'they'?"

"They, all of them. Little Alfred needs a loyal friend to guard him through the night, and Mr. Wilkens needs a bone expert to help him with his arkinsawlogy work."

"I think it's archeology."

"Please don't interrupt when I'm speaking. And last but not leashed, the lovely Sardina

Bandana needs my warm presence beside her."

He sat down, lifted his right hind leg, and began hacking at his ear. "You know, I don't think her name is Sardina. That man called her something else."

I roasted him with my eyes. "Who or whom are you going to believe: the dog who loves her or some stranger you never saw before today?"

"Well, he ought to know the name of his own dog."

"And I ought to know the name of the lady who adores me. Will you please stop scratching your ear?"

"I've got a flea."

"I don't care. Scratching is rude and very distracting. And besides, we have a long journey ahead of us."

He stopped scratching and stared at me. "We do?"

"Yes. The lake is two miles west of here, and there's some danger that we'll encounter coyotes along the way."

"Coyotes!"

"Yes, and you'll be proud to hear this." I laid a paw on his shoulder. "Drover, I've decided to move you up to the varsity. Congratulations."

The Runt Gets His
Big Chance

If you recall, I had just given Drover the great
news: I had decided to move him up to the
varsity.

His eyes crossed. "The varsity! You mean . . ."

"Yes, Drover, I think you're ready for the Big
Game. I'm going to give you the starting position
at offensive tackle. Is that exciting or what?"

His eyes grew wider. "Tackle! Me?"

"Yes sir. You'll be right up front with the big
boys. I want you to go out there and really bust
somebody, show 'em who's boss."

"I already know."

"What?"

"I said . . . varsity, oh boy. Goodie."

"That's the spirit, Drover. This could be the

biggest game of the season. Let's go get 'em!"

He jumped to his feet and let out a cheer. "Let me at 'em, I'll hammer their helmets! I'll knock their socks off and then I'll . . ." Suddenly, he went down like a rock. "Oh drat the luck, there it went! This old leg quit me again! Oh, the pain!"

"Maybe it's just a cramp."

"No, I really messed it up this time."

"Work through it, son, you're on the varsity now. The team needs you."

"I know, it's what I've always dreamed of, but I just don't think this old leg'll stay under me."

I paced a few feet away and gazed up at the sky. "Okay, here's an idea. Suppose we move *me* to offensive tackle and give *you* the starting job at running back?"

"You know, that might work."

I whirled around and gave him a scorching glare. "Just as I suspected. There's nothing wrong with your leg. Get off your lazy duff, and let's go out there and win a big one for the ranch."

"Well, okay, if you think . . ." His eyes popped wide open and he pointed at something behind me. "Oh my gosh . . . it's THEM!"

Huh? Them? I whirled to the right and went into my karate stance, expecting to see a whole herd of cannibals coming at me with flashing

142

teeth. What I saw was a whole herd of wild turkeys, clucking and pecking down along the creek.

"False alarm, Drover, it's just . . ." He had vanished. "Drover?" All that remained was a small cloud of dust above the spot where he had been sitting. "Drover! Come back here! I'm giving you a direct order! Okay, pal, if you're not back here in two minutes, you're off the team!"

From somewhere in the distance, I heard a faint cry. "Oh, my leg! Oh, the guilt!"

I couldn't believe it. Yes, I could. It was exactly what you'd expect from an ungrateful, unpatriotic, quivering little gold-bricker. I'd given him the opportunity of a lifetime, a starting position on the ranch's team, but instead of seizing the opportunity . . .

Oh well, I didn't need him anyway. I'd be better off without him. It was only a short two-mile hike over to the lake, and maybe I wouldn't run into the Coyote Brotherhood. Sure, they often hung out under the shade of the cottonwoods along the creek, but maybe today . . . gulp.

I raised my voice to a shout. "Okay, Drover, I've decided to reshuffle the starting lineup. Come back and we'll try you at running back. What an opportunity, huh?"

I cocked my ear and listened. Not a sound. No doubt he had already burrowed into the deepest, darkest corner of the machine shed and nothing less than a bulldozer could have pulled him out.

I turned my gaze to the west. Well, I would have to make this journey all alone, without an offensive line. Was I scared? Not at all. Okay, let's put it this way. Any dog in his right mind would be worried about making such a journey, so yes, I felt some concern.

To be honest, I felt pretty nervous about it, but you know what drove me onward? The picture in my mind, the glowing picture, of my beloved Sardina Bandana waving good-bye as tears splashed down her cheeks. That's the kind of vision that drives a dog to endure all kinds of danger and hardship.

Even so, there was little room for mistakes or miscalculations. Even a tiny error in navigation could land me into a confrontation with blood-thirsty cannibals and, well, we certainly didn't need that. I would have to plot my strategy down to the tiniest dovetails.

Would you be interested in seeing my plan? It's Highly Classified information but maybe it wouldn't hurt if we gave you a little peek.

Let's step into the Map Room and study a

chart of the ranch and surrounding territory. Okay, here we are at the feed shed on the west end of ranch headquarters. Directly to the west of the feed shed, we have this fence running north and south, separating the home pasture from the horse pasture.

The "home pasture" gets its name from the fact that the home of Loper and Sally May sits pretty muchly in the center of it, and the "horse pasture" was so named because . . . well, because that's where we keep the horses. If we kept black cows in that pasture, we might call it the "black cow pasture," but we don't so we don't.

It's kind of complicated but the thing to remember is that horses stay in the *horse* pasture.

Okay, notice that the creek winds its way through the horse pasture. An ordinary dog making a trek across this pasture on a scorching hot summer day would follow the creek, right? Of course he would. Why? Because trees grow along the creek and an ordinary dog would be interested in staying in the shade, sparing himself from being broiled alive in the glare of the sun.

But that brings us to the kernel of the nutshell. If dogs crave the shade of graceful cottonwood trees, who else do you suppose might be spending the afternoon loafing in the shade along the creek?

Coyotes, which is precisely why I had made my generous offer to move Drover up to the varsity. In the event that we blundered into the afternoon camp of some cannibals, having Drover up there on the offensive line would, uh, open up a few options, so to speak.

But Drover had blown that opportunity, so maybe you're beginning to see the outlines of my new game plan. Instead of following the creek, I would set a course . . . here, look at the map . . . set a course two hundred yards north of the creek. As you can see, the new course would deny me the luxury of walking in the shade, but it would also deny lounging cannibals the luxury of eating me.

Pretty shrewd, huh? You bet, and now you've had an inside look at my plan for this mission: Stick to the high ground, endure the glare of the sun, and avoid nasty confrontations with cannibals along the creek.

I was ready. I took one last compass reading from the sun and set a course of two-five-zero-zero, and marched out into the pasture. "Be brave, Sardina, your hero is coming!" I knew she wouldn't hear my call but that was okay. It made me feel braver and kind of took my mind off the heat.

And boy, it was hot! After marching the first quarter mile in the glaring sun, I was panting so

hard, I had to switch my tongue over to the left side of my mouth. Some of your town dogs and ordinary yard mutts pant with their tongues pointing straight ahead. What they don't know is that a dog can do a better job of cooling himself down when his tongue hangs out the *left side* of his mouth. It makes the old tongue look kind of like a dead fish, but so what? It works.

Anyway, it wasn't a great day to be out on a hike, but I had an excellent reason for . . . HUH?

Okay, let's pause here for just a moment to review our, uh, Marching Plans. In drawing up our plans, we had devised a clever strategy for avoiding coyotes, remember? But what you forgot to bring up in our planning sessions was that we would be trekking across the horse pasture and that horse pastures almost always contain . . . what?

Horses. Remember our previous discussions about horses? They are hateful, spiteful, arrogant, overbearing bullies who also happen to be huge, and they love to torment dogs. I mean, show 'em a badge that says you're Head of Ranch Security and they'll laugh in your face. Tell 'em that you're on a very important mission and they'll laugh even harder. Tell 'em that they're all under arrest . . .

Don't ever tell a herd of horses they're under

arrest. It will backfire every time. One dog should never threaten to arrest thirteen head of horses, each of them weighing over a thousand pounds, but you know, sometimes in a flash of anger, we say things we later regret.

This is painful. I would rather skip over it so that the little children would never know . . . I mean, how can the Head of Ranch Security preserve law and order when . . . well, when he's being chased around the pasture by thirteen head of mocking, shrieking horses whose huge teeth are trying to snap off his tail?

It was a shameful, humiliating experience, and the less we say about it, the better. Let's just say that if a dog runs in circles long enough, horses will get bored and leave. That's what happened, and as the cowards trotted away, I yelled, "And let that be a lesson to you! Get out of my horse pasture and don't ever come back!"

Told them, huh? You bet. The big bullies.

I glanced around and noticed I had moved down along the creek, only a short distance from the shade of a big cottonwood tree. I had worked up quite a sweat, so I trotted over to the . . .

Oops. Coyotes. Two of them, lying in the shade of the cottonwood tree.

Warning! This Chapter Contains Cannibal Material!

It was Rip and Snort, the very thugs I had planned to avoid, and would have avoided if the stinking horses hadn't messed up my plan. My first thought was that I had landed myself in a big mess of trouble, but then I noticed an important detail.

The brothers didn't look their usual selves—not fearsome and ferocious but wilted, worn out, and bedraggled. They were lying in the shade, see, and hardly moving, panting for air while their tongues dripped water and their eyes held me in a listless gaze.

All at once, a bold thought popped into my mind. "I think I can talk my way out of this." So instead of trying to run away, as most of your ordinary mutts would have done, I switched on a pleasant smile. "Hey, Rip and Snort, great to see you again! How's it going? Beautiful day, huh?"

With great effort, Snort mumbled, "Dutiful day for dummy ranch dog. Not so dutiful for coyote brothers."

"Really? Gee, what seems to be the problem?"

"Day too hotter and hottest for coyote wearing fur coat."

I moved closer and studied their wooden eyes. "Yes, I see what you mean. Snort, I hate to tell you this, but you guys look awful."

"Hunk not look so wonderful, too."

"Right. It's this heat. And you know, fellas, on a day like today, the last thing a guy would ever think about is . . . well, food. Eating. Am I right about that?" No response. "I mean, just think about eating a piece of dry cornbread when your mouth is already parched."

"Hunk not talk about cornbread. Make Snort's mouth feel like bag of dirt."

"Right, that's what I mean. It's way too hot and dry to be thinking about crumbly powdery CORNBREAD."

Snort shot me a killer look, rose to his feet, and rumbled over to me. "Hunk shut trap and not talk about dry stuff when coyote brothers got big boom-boom thirsty in mouth!"

"Well, sure. I was just . . ."

Up came his right paw and he clubbed me over the head. BONK! "Hunk shut trap."

"I can handle that, and besides, I need to be getting along anyway." I began edging toward the west. "I'm starting a new job and, well, I wouldn't want to be late."

"Ha, ha, ha!"

"No, I'm serious. Showing up late on the first day would be no laughing matter."

"Ha ha ha!"

"But you keep laughing."

"Maybe Hunk stick around for supper, oh boy."

"Supper? In this heat? Who could think about . . . listen, maybe we could discuss this another time. What do you say?"

They said nothing, just stared at me and ran their respective tongues over their chops. I was getting a bad feeling about this and decided that it might be a good time to test out our new Turbo Six application. I reached for the throttle and pushed it to the Blast Off Position. The engines screamed and I went zooming . . .

BAM!

Up to that very moment, the brothers had

seemed as lifeless as rocks, but when I reached for the throttle, they sprang into action and blocked my path. I hit 'em with a full head of steam. It was like a gnat hitting a barn door.

Snort raised his lips and showed me two rows of gleaming fangs. "Hunk stick around till cool of evening when coyote feel more hungry for eat."

I coughed and struggled to my feet. "Oh. Well, since you put it that way . . . sure, what the heck." I turned away from them so they couldn't see the fear in my eyes. I mean, this deal had taken a big turn for the worse and I didn't want them thinking that I was . . . well, scared out of my wits, which I was.

So I turned my face toward the south and suddenly realized that I was looking at a very important piece of information that had escaped me up to then: THE CREEK HAD GONE DRY.

Do you see the meaning of this? Maybe not, but I did, and a new plan began taking shape in the vast caverns of my mind. "So you guys are thirsty? Is that what you said?"

"Guys got big boom-boom thirsty in mouth."

"Well, gee whiz, why don't you just get a drink?"

The brothers hacked out a jagged laugh, and Snort pointed toward the creek. "Creek gone dry, gee whiz no water."

"Well, sure, but what about root beer?" They gave me empty stares. "You don't know about the root beer deposits below the sand?" More blank stares. "Oh, well, I'm sorry I mentioned it. You'd probably think it was too much trouble anyway. Don't give it a thought."

The brothers went into a whispering conference, then Snort said, "Brothers not believe in root beer."

"That's fine, Snort. We can still be friends, even though you don't believe in root beer."

They whispered some more, then, "Ranch dog tell Rip and Snort about root beer."

"How can I tell you about root beer if you don't believe in it?"

Snort came rumbling over to me and showed me a clenched paw. "Snort believe in break Hunk's face. Talk!"

"All right, but you don't need to be so hateful about it." I launched into a long discussion about how, in periods of drought, the creeks run dry and all the sweetness of the earth flows out of tree roots below the sand and forms vast reserves of root beer. "All you have to do is dig down into the sand and you'll strike root beer."

They howled with laughter and whopped each

other on the back. "Hunk tell pretty funny story, but Rip and Snort not believe one word."

"Well, that's fine. I didn't want to share it anyway. I mean, you guys may be bigger and stronger and faster than me, but don't forget that this is still my ranch—my ranch, my roots, and my root beer."

Behind my back, I could hear them whispering and a moment later, Snort loomed up beside me. He pointed toward the creek bed. "Hunk dig."

"Yes, but you said . . ."

"Hunk dig! And better find root beer pretty quick, oh boy!"

He gave me a shove and stood over me while I started digging. "Snort, don't expect miracles. These things take time." I dug and dug. Ten minutes passed, and I had built a hole maybe two feet deep.

Snort stared into the hole and made a sour face. "Sand still dry. Hunk dig faster."

"Hey listen, it's hot out here. I'm digging as fast as I can."

I dug some more, while Snort sniffed the sand for signs of moisture. Three feet down, I was still pulling up dry sand, and I'll bet you're starting to worry. Maybe you're thinking: "Hank's really done it this time, telling the cannibal brothers a big whopper about root beer under the ground."

Good point. I mean, never make a cannibal mad before suppertime, right? That's good advice, the kind of common sense wisdom that can help a dog live a long and happy life. But here's the scoop. There was one particle of truth in the story. In the heat of summer, the creek sometimes goes dry, but you can always find wet sand, and sometimes even water, if you dig down far enough.

Now do you see where this is going? If not, just sit back and enjoy the show. I'm pretty sure you'll be impressed.

Okay, I was digging a root-beer well in the middle of the dry creek bed on a very hot afternoon. Rip and Snort were about to die of thirst and stood over the hole, broiling in the sun and getting more impatient by the second.

At last, I hit some wet sand. "Here we go, guys, we're almost there!"

Snort sniffed the wet sand and beamed a wicked grin. "Hunk better hurry up quick or brothers get madder and maddest!"

"Snort, I'm digging just as fast as I can."

"Ha! Hunk dig like snail, slower than slow."

"For your information, pal, I'm the fastest

digger I ever met, and the fastest digger on this whole ranch." The brothers roared with laughter. "Oh yeah? Do you know anybody who could dig faster?"

Snort stuck his nose close to my face. "Hunk dig like flea. Snort faster diggest in whole world, oh boy!"

Rip scowled, shook his head and grunted, "Uh-uh!" He pointed to himself, as if to say that he was the fastest digger in the whole world.

Snort made a sour face and glared down at me. "Hunk get out of hole."

"What? Are you crazy? I started drilling this well and I'm going to take it all the way down to root beer, and no fleabag coyote is going to . . ."

In the blink of an eye, Snort darted his head into the hole, snapped his jaws around the scruff of my neck, jerked me out of the hole, and tossed me aside like stuffed toy.

Then he pounded his chest with both front paws and roared, "Now Hunk watch Snort dig up whole world!"

But while Snort was pounding his chest, Rip dived head-first into the hole and started moving dirt, only by then it was mud. The first plop of mud hit Snort right in the mouth and there for a second, I thought he was going to hurt somebody, either me or his brother. But then he smacked his lips and a big silly grin spread across his mouth.

"Uh! Root beer! Berry good for fix up boom-boom thirsty!" And with that, he leaped high in the air and dived into the hole. Dove. Diven. Phooey.

I could have told him that one hole in the sand, dug by one dog, isn't big enough to hold two cannibals, but he didn't ask and you can guess what happened next. All at once we had two coyotes wedged into a hole, and two sets of coyote legs cranking around like they were pedaling a bicycle, but without the bicycle.

And there was a bunch of noise coming from the bottom of that hole.

Well, this seemed a pretty good time for me to move along, but I couldn't resist giving them one last good-bye. "How does it look, guys? Any sign of root beer yet? No? Well, darn the luck. Hey listen, if you make it to Australia, maybe some-body'll bring you a glass of iced tea. See you around, suckers. Ha ha ha!"

You know, sometimes Security Work can fall into a dull routine, but there's nothing dull about yelling, "See you around, suckers," to a couple of helpless, stranded coyotes in a hole.

Wow! I loved it and went skipping off to my new assignment as Chief Arkinsawlogist of the

Entire Wolf Creek District of Texas. What a great day to be a dog!

Of course there was one tiny problem with this incident. Once you've served up a smashing defeat to a couple of cannibals, you need to avoid them for a while. I mean, those guys are a few bales short of a full load of brains, but they're bad about carrying a grudge.

Maybe I shouldn't have called them suckers. Maybe I should have just walked away and kept my mouth shut. When you're a winner, you don't need to brag or boast or gloast, even though it's great fun.

I reached for the notepad of my mind and scratched down a message. "Avoid all coyotes for six months."

There! It was done and now I could turn my full attention to my new job assignment and . . . mercy, I had almost forgotten about her in all the excitement. The lovely Sardina Bandana. My mind pulled up a photograph of her as she was leaving my ranch, weeping rivers of tears and calling out my name.

I felt a new wave of energy coursing through my body. "Fear not, O Beloved, your Hank has fought his way through the cannibal armies and is coming to save you!"

CHAPTER SIXTEEN

I Start My New Job

The rest of the journey went off without a hitch and I hardly even noticed the heat. Okay, I noticed the heat, but I was so pumped up about the new direction my life had taken that I didn't let it bother me.

The dig site was easy to find. I could see it half a mile away: six or seven pickups and cars parked in a row beside a collection of tents that looked like flowers in the distance, red and blue and green against a background of drab yellow grass.

I rolled into camp around three o'clock and . . . you know, I had sort of expected a welcoming committee—not anything fancy, but maybe two or three of their top people who would drop their digging tools and rush out to welcome me. I mean, how often does a Head of Ranch Security show up at these deals?

Nobody even noticed I was there! Oh well. I tried not to get my feelings hurt. I knew they were busy, and to be fair about it, a lot of those folks didn't realize who I was.

Do we need to do a quick review of what's involved in an arkinsawlogy dig? Maybe so, and we can start with the correct pronunciation of the word. It's *archeology*, not arkinsawlogy. I don't know who started calling it arkinsawlogy . . . well, yes I do.

Drover, and that should come as no great surprise. The runt has trouble remembering his own name, much less big scientific words like arkinsawlogy.

Archeology.

Archeologists dig around in the dirt and look for old things, but they don't do it with backhoes or even with shovels. No sir, when I got there, I saw seven grown men on their knees, humped over like snails and dragging trowels across patches of dirt that were as square and flat as wooden boxes.

This was the "site." That's what they called it, the site, and they had it laid out in several squares that were marked by string lines. The digging took place in the shade provided by a big blue awning, a kind of tent, open at the sides and held up by poles that were anchored in the ground by ropes and stakes.

They would trowel for a while, then scoop up the dirt and toss it into a white plastic bucket. When a bucket got full, a tall fellow named Mike picked it up and carried it to a screen. He wore a cowboy straw hat and had a silver mustache, and he would dump the bucket of dirt into the screen and shake it back and forth until all the loose dirt had fallen through.

Then he would bend over the screen and pick out certain objects that he called "cultural material": pieces of bone, charcoal, pottery, and flint, which he dropped into a small paper sack with writing on it.

At the same time, Dave Wilkens was walking around, looking down into all the holes. He would pull on his chin and say, "Hmmmm," and write something on his clipboard. No kidding, that was it. I have no idea what he was writing down, but maybe it was just "hmmmm."

Well! After sitting quietly and observing it all for fifteen minutes, and listening to ten thousand wasps buzzing overhead, I began to realize that this was REALLY BORING. So, to liven things up a bit, I took in a big gulp of air and delivered a loud bark that said, "Hey fellas, great news. *I'm here!*"

Yipes. It didn't exactly liven things up. It stopped everything dead in its tracks. I mean, every head came up and every eye swung around to me, and, fellers, the silence that fell over the place was almost scary. Then Mr. Wilkens said, "Hey, Slim, some of your kinfolks just showed up."

Up till then, I hadn't seen Slim or Alfred, but now their heads popped out of one of the holes. When Slim saw me, he chuckled. "Kinfolks. Wilkie, you have a sick mind."

Alfred's eyes grew wide and he gasped, "Hankie! What are you doing here?"

Well, I . . . I glanced around at all the frozen faces and all the narrowed eyes, and all at once I felt that we should discuss this in private. I mean, I didn't know these people and they didn't seem quite as thrilled about my presence as they should have been. So I trotted over to the hole where he . . .

"Watch the string line!"

Oops. Okay, they had yellow string lines all over the place, and maybe I tripped over one of them. What was the deal with all the string? I mean, it was like some kind of giant booby trap. If they didn't want dogs tripping over their string

164

lines, they should have . . . I don't know, put them somewhere else.

Anyway, I trotted over to the hole where Slim and the boy were . . . well, doing whatever they were doing.

Alfred didn't look happy. "Hankie, Mom said she was going to lock you up in the barn."

My eyes drifted up to the clouds. Yes, well, his mom and I discussed that and we decided that on a normal day, I'd rather not be locked in a barn . . . and she wasn't fast enough to catch me.

The boy shook his finger in my face. "Hankie, you're a naughty dog." He glared at me for a moment. I began sending up Looks of Remorse and it wasn't long until he grinned. "But I'm kind of glad you came, 'cause now we can sleep together in the tent."

Hey, that sounded like good wholesome entertainment, a boy and his dog sharing the great outdoors.

I dived into the hole and said hello to Slim. I figured he would be happy to see me. I mean, who wouldn't be thrilled to see an old friend? (We weren't actually kinfolks. I think that was some kind of joke.)

But he didn't act so thrilled. "Hank, get out of my unit!"

What unit? I turned to see what he was yelling about and somehow my tail knocked over his bucket.

"Dog, for all I know, you might be standing on top of King Tut. Scram!"

Me? Standing on top of . . . gee, I couldn't see anything but dirt. Maybe he was talking to someone else, but his face sure was turning red and I could see the blood vessels standing out on his forehead when he brought his angry face right up to mine and hissed, "Will you please get out of my unit?"

Well, he'd said "please," so we seemed to be making progress. I figured this might be a good time to extend the hand of friendship, so I offered him a paw to shake. Maybe that was a bad idea. He jacked himself up to a standing position (and did a lot of groaning in the process) and pitched— I mean, physically *threw* me—out of his hole . . . unit . . . whatever you call it.

Gee whiz, he didn't need to yell and screech, and what was the big deal anyway? As far as I could tell, he was raving about DIRT. How much dirt did he need? If he didn't want to share that patch of dirt, why couldn't he go somewhere else? I mean, there's a whole lot of dirt in this world, and it's a sad day when a grown man gets so fussy that he can't share a little piece of it with a loyal dog.

Oh well. I had already begun to suspect that people who spend entire days scratching around in the dirt are . . . how can I say this? They're just a little bit strange, and for his information, I had no wish to spend another second in his so-called "unit" (it was nothing but dirt, honest).

Mr. Wilkens drifted over and gave Slim a looking-over. "You look kind of stiff."

"Yeah, my body wasn't meant to be folded up in a hole. My knees hurt, my back hurts, everything hurts."

There was no sympathy in Wilkens' face. "I guess you've been living a pampered life. You'll get used to the pain." Wilkens knelt down, looked into Slim's unit, and pointed toward some kind of lump in the middle. "What is that?"

"Well, it looks like the top of a rock to me."

"What's your elevation?" When Slim didn't answer, Wilkie looked up at him. "What's your elevation?"

"Well, I was six foot tall till that horse throwed me through the west wall of the saddle shed, and I s'pect I'm some shorter now."

Wilkie's eyes grew distant. "Slim, what is the elevation in your unit? How deep are you?"

"Oh." Slim frowned and looked into the hole. "Well, that's hard to say. You want me to guess?"

"Slim, this is science. We don't guess. We measure." Wilkie pitched him a measuring tape. "Use the string level, and measure down from there."

Slim pulled out the tape and squinted at it. "Good honk, did you notice all these weird little lines?"

"Yes. They're centimeters. We use metric units."

"You know, I got stung by a centimeter one time and it hurt for three days."

Wilkie laughed and shook his head. "Slim, step down into the unit and measure your elevation."

"Do I have to use all them little marks on the tape measure?"

"Yes."

Slim heaved a sigh. "This is worse than brain surgery." He got down in the hole and told Alfred to pull the string level—a string with a level hanging from it—tight. When the bubble meddled in the lid of the settle . . . settled in the middle of the level, Slim pulled out a strip of tape, set the end of it on the floor of the unit, and squinted at the marks on the tape.

"Well, it says . . . it says either fifty or fifty thousand or five hundred million, I can't tell which."

Wilkie rubbed his chin. "Fifty centimeters. You ought to be pretty close to the floor of the house, but the north wall is over there." He pointed to another unit. "That's where you'd expect to find a big rock. What's it doing in the middle of the house?"

Little Alfred said, "Maybe it's a dinosaur bone."

Wilkens smiled. "Believe me, it's not a dinosaur bone. Not in these parts." He turned back to Slim. "Well, take your unit on down and leave the rock in place. When you get down to sixty centimeters, we'll take another look at it."

"Can I use a shovel?"

"A shovel? Ha ha."

"Will I have to measure again?"

"Yes."

"When's quitting time?"

Wilkens strolled away. "Midnight."

"Wilkens, you're even crueler and more heartless than High Loper, and that's nothing to be proud of." To no one in particular, Slim muttered, "This archeology reminds me of a cold. Just when you think it can't get worse, it gets worse."

Nobody was listening to his complaints, so he went down on his knees again, folded up his legs, and started scraping dirt with a trowel. Little

Alfred did the same, but with less grumbling.

Scrape, scrape. Pick, pick. Brush, brush. Ho hum. Time sure did crawl. I sat for a while, laid down for a while, yawned three times, scratched two fleas, and took another yawn. Ho hum. But at last, some excitement appeared on the scenery.

A grasshopper landed right in front of me. You know, on an ordinary day, I don't get excited about grasshoppers. Drover does but I don't. But this was turning out to be a pretty slow day, so I flipped the switch for Slow Hydraulic Lift, rose to my feet, and began inching my nose toward the hateful grasshopper. When he flew... well, maybe I tried to, fly too, only...

"Hank, for crying out loud!"

Okay, maybe I'd gotten absorbed in the grasshopper and had forgotten about . . . well, Slim and the hole and so forth, and I flew right on top of his back. Anyway, I got his attention. "Alfred, call your dog and get 'im out of here."

Alfred climbed out of the hole and called me. I leaped out of the hole and followed him away from Slim's crummy little playpen. By George, if he didn't want my help, that was fine. I had better things to do, and he could just . . . I don't know, suffer through life without me.

What a grouch.

CHAPTER SEVENTEEN

Sardina's Weird Sister

As the boy and I marched away from Slim's hole in the ground, he wagged a finger at me. "Hankie, you've got to stay away from the estivation."

Estivation? Oh, *excavation*. Got it.

"You know what we're digging up?"

Well, uh, not exactly. It looked pretty muchly like dirt to me.

"It's a house."

A house? No kidding? I strained my eyes to see the things you normally expect to see in a house, such as walls, a roof, a front porch, furniture, potted plants . . . but I couldn't see much of anything.

"It's old, old, old, Hankie, and it's been buried

under dirt for a long time. All that's left is some wocks. See that?" He pointed toward an area where several men were digging, a line of caliche rocks that had been exposed during the dig. "That was a wall, see? It's part of the house. Pwetty neat, huh?"

Rocks. Well, to be honest, I had never thought of rocks as being very exciting, but if a guy had to choose between playing with rocks and playing with dirt, maybe he could get worked up about a couple of dozen rocks.

It wasn't my place to judge or offer opinions, but in the privacy of my own mind, I heard a voice say, "It sure doesn't take much to entertain a bunch of archeologists."

Alfred moved on down to the south end of the estivation . . . excavation . . . and pointed to a man who was working in one of the units. He was curled up in a ball with all his weight resting on his knees, so that his hind end was up in the air and his nose was down close to the level of the ground.

What was he doing down there? In one hand he held a little stick of wood and in the other a small brush. He picked dirt with the stick and brushed it away with . . . well, with the brush, of course.

Mr. Wilkens drifted over to us. "That's Doug

McGrubber, and he's trying to expose a large piece of bison bone. We think it might be a tibia digging stick."

Bone? My ears shot up and my tongue swept across my lips. Hey, this was getting more interesting.

"It was a digging tool. Prehistoric people used a bone that came from the leg of a buffalo. They lashed it to a stick and used it for cultivating their corn. Doug wants to take it out in one piece and that's why he's being so careful."

Oh. Well, old Doug was being plenty careful, all right, not to mention slower than grandma. I found myself staring into the trench and, uh, admiring his bone.

Slurp.

Huh? All of a sudden, Doug McGrubber straightened up and turned a pair of dark eyes on me, and in a spooky tone of voice, he muttered, "Don't you even think about it, Shep."

Me? What had I . . . had I said anything about bothering his bone? Was there some law against a dog having a private thought now and then? I mean, this was still America and we dogs had rights, too.

And my name wasn't Shep.

I found it convenient to, uh, move my freight a

few steps to the south and take up a new position behind Mr. Wilkens' legs, out of the spotlight of Doug McGrubber's glare.

Were my thoughts so transparent? If so, I would have to make some changes. I mean, when you're in Security Work, you need a face that says nothing, a face that can keep dark secrets, such as ... well, that was a very interesting bone.

I would keep my distance from Doug McGrubber. The guy gave me the creeps.

As I said, I had taken up a position behind Mr. Wilkens' legs, but maybe he didn't know it, and when he turned to walk away, he ... well, he stumbled. Tripped over me, you might say, and came within a hair of plunging to the ground.

He looked down at me with a forced smile. "Hank, I've got a great idea. How would you like to go sit in the shade of the pickups?"

You know, I was pretty content where I was, right in the middle of ...

"Hank, leave!"

Well, sure. Hey, I had no problem moving over to the shade of the pickups. No, I take that back. Actually, the change of location did present me with one problem. If I was sitting in the shade of the pickups, far from the center of the action, how could I do a proper job of supervising the work?

Maybe Wilkie thought he could handle things without me. That kind of hurt my feelings, but as you will soon see, I found other things to hold my interest. Wow!

Mr. Wilkens and Little Alfred escorted me over to the line of vehicles that were parked just south of the estivation site . . . excavation site, let us say, and I must be honest and say that I had a feeling that I got the escort service because . . . well, because they didn't trust me. I heard them talking, see.

Alfred: "He really tries to be a good dog."

Mr. Wilkens: "I'm sure he does, but he'll be happier over here, out of everyone's way. And the crew will be a lot happier."

"Can he stay the night?"

"We'll wait and see. Maybe . . . if he minds his manners."

There, you see? The guy hardly knew me and yet he was already lumping me in with all the other mutts in the world who have no manners and can't be trusted to control their behavior. It kind of wounded my pride, to tell you the truth, but . . . oh well, I would just have to prove that I was a different kind of dog.

I followed them to the line of vehicles, where Mr. Wilkens pointed to a shady spot near the back of his white Chevy pickup. "Stay here, Hank."

Yes sir. I went straight into the requisite Three-Turns-and-Flop Maneuver and settled into my spot in the shade. Little Alfred waved good-bye, and they returned to the dig.

Ho hum. Heat waves danced on the horizon and wasps droned in the air. Five minutes later, I was dying of boredom. This wasn't going to be fun. But then . . . I heard a sound coming from the pickup above me. I rose to my feet and glanced around.

"Hello? Is someone there?" I cocked my ear and listened.

And I heard a lady's voice say, "Oh. It's you."

"I beg your pardon? Who are you and where are you?" She stepped into my viewpoint and I saw her face, looking down at me from the pickup bed, and what a glorious face it was! It was the kind of face that sends a dog's heart crashing down to his feet, then roaring up to his head like . . . I don't know what. Like an elevator gone wild, like a skyrocket out of control.

My eyes popped wide open. "Holy smokes, Sardina Bandana!"

"My name is *Saffron*, and we've already had this conversation. What's wrong with you?"

I leaped to my feet and gazed up at her. "There must be some mistake. I met a lady dog this

177

morning but her name was Sardina Bandana, and I can assure you, madame, she wasn't even half as beautiful as you. You're gorgeous!"

She rolled her eyes. "Her name was Saffron and she was ME."

I had to chuckle. "Ha ha. Okay, you're playing some little game here and you want me to play along. Very well, let me guess." I paced a few steps away, then whirled around. "You and Sardina are best friends, am I right?" She didn't answer. "Okay, let's try again. You and Sardina are sisters and you're playing a joke."

She stared at me for what seemed a whole minute before a little smile curled at the corners of her mouth. "You're pretty observant, aren't you?"

"Hey, that's my business. Did I mention that I'm Head of Ranch Security?"

"Really! Head of Ranch Security. Is that as important as it sounds?"

"Oh yes ma'am. I'm not one to brag but, well, you're talking to the guy who barks up the sun every day."

She was stunned. "No, honestly? You're the one?"

"Yes ma'am, the very one. And when I'm not barking up the sun and providing sunshine for all

178

the little children, I'm busting monsters and solving mysteries."

She let out a giggle. "Oh my, and I thought I could fool you."

"Heh heh. Well, a lot of 'em try, ma'am, but I'm always one step ahead. See, I knew right away that you and Sardina were sisters."

She gave her head a shake. "Well, this is just amazing. Would you like to speak to Sardina?"

"Well . . . sure, why not? I mean, if one gal is good, two are double good, right?"

She gave me a wink. "She's right over here. Don't go away."

She stepped out of my view and I heard myself say, "Me, go away? Lady, you don't know me as well as I know me. Heh heh. I wouldn't miss this for all the bones in Texas."

A moment later, Sardina Bandana made her appearance, a lady dog of such gasperating beauty that I could hardly breathe. When I finally found my voice, I stammered, "Holy smokes, you're gorgeous!"

She primped at her ears. "Oh foo. You probably don't even remember me."

"Ha! I remember you very well, my sugar plum. You come from Boston, you enjoy swimming in the ocean, and you hate lobsters. When they carried you away from my ranch this morning, I saw the tears streaming down your cheeks."

"You did?"

"I did. And Sardina, my dumpling, ever since that moment, I haven't been able to eat or sleep or think about anything but you."

Her smile vanished. "Oh? I heard you talking to Saffron, and you said *she* was gorgeous."

"Me? I said that?"

She turned two flaming eyes at me. "You certainly did, and how do you suppose that makes me feel? You probably go around saying that to all the girls."

"I don't."

"You're a cad!"

"I'm not. I'm the sweetest, kindest dog I've ever met, honest."

She lifted her chin. "Then prove it. Choose one of us, me or my sister. You can't have both of us."

I paced a few steps away, gathering my thoughts. "Very well, if you insist. Sardina, when I first laid eyes on your sister, I thought she was gorgeous, but now that I've seen you again, I know that I was wrong."

"You're sure?"

"Absolutely. Next to you, a blooming rose is but a pitiful thing."

"Oh, how sweet! You've chosen me?"

"Yes, and congratulations, my little cherry cobbler."

She smiled and batted her eyelashes. "I'll get Saffron and you can tell her the bad news."

"Huh? No, wait . . ."

She dashed off toward the front of the pickup and a moment later . . . oops. Sackron . . . Snaffron . . . whatever her sister's name was . . . stormed into view, and fellers, she looked steamed.

CHAPTER EIGHTEEN

Never Mess with
a Dog Named
Choo Choo

Sardina's twin sister scorched me with a couple of wild eyeballs and screamed, "What? I'm uglier than a mud fence? Is that what you told my sister?"

"I . . . I . . . I didn't say anything about a mud fence, honest."

"She said you did, and you know what I'm going to do?"

"Uh . . . no."

She leaned toward me and said, "I'm going to tell my big brother!"

She vanished. Before I could speculate about what her big brother might add to the drama,

Sardina returned, shaking her head. "What did you say to my sister?"

"Well, not much, but it really seemed to get her nose out of joint."

"Did you say that she was uglier than a toad sitting on a mud fence?"

"What? No!"

"You shouldn't have said that."

"I didn't!"

"Saffron is very sensitive and, well, you've crushed her spirit, calling her names."

"I didn't call her anything!"

Sardina lowered her voice. "I guess you know what's going to happen now."

"Well . . . she said something about a brother."

She gave her head a solemn nod. "Have you met Choo Choo?"

I swallowed a lump in my throat. "Choo Choo? No. Is he big?"

"Like a train. HUGE. And he has . . . problems."

"Problems?"

"He breaks things."

"Things?"

"Trees. Furniture. Fireplugs. Dogs."

"Good grief! Do you think I can whip him?"

"Ha ha ha ha!"

I found myself glancing over both shoulders

and backing away. "Well, you tell the big ape that he can have a piece of me anytime he wants. Tell him I'll be waiting for him up in Windmill Canyon, five miles north of here. And tell him to bring his own casket—a small one because there won't be much left of him when the fight's over."

"Oh, you're so brave!" she gasped, holding her paws together. "Will I be seeing you again?"

"Let me check my schedule, and I'll get back to you."

I turned and walked away in a slow, dignified manner. Okay, maybe I didn't walk away in a dignified manner. I RAN. Would Sardina and I be seeing each other again? Not a chance. What a weird family! I mean, Sardina was gorgeous, but the sister seemed a little daffy, and the brother . . . I hadn't met him yet, but already I didn't like him. Any dog named Choo Choo was a dog I didn't need to meet.

Anyway, I spent the next three hours hiding under a Jeep, as far away from Sardina and her family as I could get. Now and then, I would peek around the left rear tire to see if the brother had showed up. I didn't see him, but when Sardina caught glimpses of me, she waved and blew kisses in my direction. She was begging me to come back, but that was too bad.

It seems cruel to put it this way, but Sardina's good looks didn't quite make up for the weirdness of her kinfolks. She could find herself another boyfriend.

I thought those three hours would never end. It was boring beyond description. Oh, there was one little flurry of excitement around five o'clock. A lazy wasp landed on Doug McGrubber's elevated bohunkus, and he made the mistake of slapping it with his trowel.

Heh heh. Never slap a lazy wasp with your trowel. It will only make the wasp angry and he will drill you every time. Heh heh. Doug McGrubber thought he was pretty smart, but I guess he wasn't as smart as the wasp that stung him. Tee hee. I kind of enjoyed it.

McGrubber howled with pain and leaped out of his unit, rubbing the injured part. "That does it! I've had enough of these stinging little monsters."

At that point, Slim Chance climbed out of his hole. He was wearing a grin. "Let not your heart be troubled. I've got a cure for them wasps."

The whole crew took a break and waited to see what kind of "cure" old Slim had up his sieve. Minutes later, he returned, carrying a dishpan filled with . . . something. Water? I couldn't see.

Mr. Wilkens drifted over and looked into the pan. "What's that?"

"This is a cowboy wasp trap: soapy water. The soap breaks the surface tension. When the wasps land on it, they sink and drown. It works."

"That simple? How'd you figure that out?"

Slim flashed a sly grin. "Well, I didn't need a tape measure and a string level, we can start there." He tapped himself on the temple. "Son, a country boy *will* survive."

You know what? It actually worked. The pan of water drew every wasp in the neighborhood. When they landed on the surface, they sank like rocks. That was the end of the Wasp Crisis and Slim became a hero around camp . . . as incredible as that seems.

And speaking of rocks, by the end of the day, Slim and Alfred had pretty muchly exposed that rock in the center of their unit. Remember the rock? Earlier in the day, Wilkie had wondered why it was located away from the walls, in a spot where you wouldn't expect to find a large rock. Now that Slim and Alfred had scraped all the soil away from it, Wilkie was even more perplexed.

Sitting on the edge of Slim's unit, he tugged on his chin and studied the rock. "Why would prehistoric people have left a big rock sitting on the floor, in the middle of their house?" Wilkie looked closer. "And you know, it's not a normal caliche rock. It looks different."

Slim nodded. "It almost looks like . . . well, a tooth or something."

"Yes, but it's way too big to be a tooth."

Little Alfred had been listening. "Maybe it's a dinosaur tooth."

Wilkie laughed.

Around seven o'clock, the crew quit for supper. Let the record show that after getting off to a shaky start, I had spent the entire afternoon being a Perfect Dog. I mean, I hadn't dived into any holes, stepped on any Egyptian mummies, stumbled over any string lines, or had any violent encounters with Sardina's brother.

I hadn't even cast longing gazes at Doug McGrubber's precious buffalo bone . . . although . . . hmmm. Maybe we should just drop the subject. As you will see, I still had some unfinished business with McGrubber's bone, but . . . never mind.

Let the record state that I had notched up a record of perfect behavior and had earned the right to remain in camp for the night, and I'm proud to report that Mr. Wilkens agreed.

When the crew quit for supper, he and Little Alfred drifted over to the Jeep, in whose shade I had spent the afternoon. Wilkie peered down at me. "Alfred, your dog conducted himself like a gentleman this afternoon. Do you think we can trust him to stay in the tent tonight?"

He gave me a hard-edged look, so I did what dogs have done since the dawn of time. I gave him Loyal Eyes, Earnest Ears, and Slow Taps on the tail section, as if to say, "All I want in this life is to become the dog you want me to be, no kidding."

I held my breath and waited.

Alfred said, "I think he'll be good."

"Well, okay. We'll give it a try. He can stay in the tent with you and Slim."

Alfred's gaze went up to the sky. "Okay . . . but Swim doesn't have a tent. All he brought was a blanket."

Wilkie shook his head. "Of course. The Cowboy Way. Son, if it rains, you'll get soaked. You want to camp with me?"

Alfred grinned and nodded. "Yes sir, 'cause Swim snores. What about my doggie?"

Mr. Wilkens gave me a hard look. I held my breath. "Okay, we'll give it a try."

Hey, perfect! They were putting me in the boss's tent. Already I had gotten a promotion, and this was still my first day.

We joined the crew for supper. They had

brought out camp chairs and placed them in a circle around a campfire. A tall skinny fellow named Witt brought out a sack of sandwich makings. He wore cutoff jeans and had a pair of bony legs that would have shamed a stork. He dumped the contents of the sack onto a small camp table and grumbled, "Here's the grub, make your own, the cook's on vacation."

My ears leaped up. Hmmm! Ham, cheese, mustard, and bread. Well, sure, you bet. I moved toward the ham.

"Not you, dog."

Huh? Well, sure, no problem. I mean, they'd been working all day in the heat and they deserved to go first.

I plopped myself down beside Mr. Witt and watched him build a huge sandwich: bread, a thick layer of mustard, two slices of ham, and that ham sure smelled good, two slices of cheese, two more slices of ham, and you know, nothing smells better at suppertime than sliced ham, and when he opened his mouth to take the first snap, my tongue swept across my mouth and I heard odd groaning sounds coming from somewhere deep inside my body.

His eyes came up and skewered me. "No."

No what? I hadn't asked for anything. Hey,

I'm no beggar, and if he didn't want to share his sandwich, that was just fine. I had better things to do than sit there and listen to him slurp and slobber.

I left and moved on around the circle . . . shopping, shall we say, and checking out the various food groups on display. Hmmm! All at once, my nose caught a pleasant aroma of something . . . well, you might describe it as a deep nutty smell—not "nutty" in the sense of being crazy, but nutty in the sense of smelling like . . . well, nuts, roasted nuts.

I fine-turned the settings on Snifforadar and traced the aroma to . . . oops, Doug McGrubber, the same guy who'd accused me of staring at his bone. To be honest, he had struck me as gripey, crabby, and generally unpleasant, but . . . well, he was eating something that smelled pretty yummy, so I decided that he might have qualities of spirit, let us say, that I hadn't noticed before.

I mean, we should never make quick judgments about a person, just because he has a lousy personality.

I sat down beside him and waited to be recognized. He held a slice of bread in his left hand and with his right, he smeared the bread with a thick layer of something brown. I inched closer and began taking air samples, and yes, the good smell seemed to be coming from whatever he was putting on the bread.

He added a second slice of bread, opened his mouth like a crocodile, and, good grief, took a huge bite out of it. How many bites could a poor sandwich take and still survive? I inched closer and licked my chops.

His eyes swung around and drilled me. "Don't give me them eyes, Shep. I don't want to hear about it."

Eyes? What was he talking about. Slurp.

He chewed and swallowed and leaned toward me. "You want a bite of this peanut butter sandwich, right?"

Well . . . okay, the thought had occurred to me, although I hadn't actually known that it was peanut butter. But now that he'd brought up the subject . . . it did smell pretty good.

He grinned. "See? I can read you like a billboard, like one of them big electric signs in Las Vegas. It says," he swept his hand around in a big circle, "*'Gimme a bite, I love peanut butter!'* Now, tell me if I'm wrong."

Gee, was it so obvious?

He gave me a wink. "But here's something you don't know. You really don't want this sandwich."

How could he say that? I knew me well enough to know that I wanted it very much. If I didn't get a bite or two, why, I might just wither up and die.

"No, you don't want it, or you shouldn't, and here's why. Pay attention." He leaned closer and dropped his voice to a creepy whisper. You won't believe what he said.

CHAPTER NINETEEN

Stricken with Tongue Hungalosis

What he said was one of the dumbest, most ridiculous things I'd ever heard! You won't believe this. I sure didn't. Here's what he said, and this is a direct quote. He said, "Dogs can't chew peanut butter."

I stared at him. WHAT? Dogs can't chew peanut butter? That was pure rubbish. Dogs chew bones all the time, and even sticks when we're bored, and if we can chew bones and sticks, who's afraid of peanut butter?

Absurd. Ridiculous. And to underscore the point, I inched closer to him and put on an awesome display of Yearning: moved my paws up and down, lifted my ears, fluttered my eyelids, moaned, and even sent a quiver through my entire body. Yes sir, all of that at the same time. It was pretty amazing.

He flashed a wicked grin. "Shep, don't want what you shouldn't want. You'd be disappointed, take my word for it."

My whole body quivered with desire.

McGrubber shook his head and glanced around the circle. The other men were watching and waiting to see which of us would win this debate. Suddenly I realized that his sandwich was there in front of my nose . . . and he wasn't watching.

Did I want a bite? No, but I would take the whole thing. SNARF! Tee hee. I snatched it out of his hand and disappeared. Foolish man.

Well, why not? I could see that the argument wasn't getting us anywhere, and what did he expect? Hold a samwish in frump of a schtarving gog and only a dunce would pect him to sit there . . . lum mum lum . . . izpeck him to zit there . . . lumble mumble lum mum . . .

You know, I'd never tried to eat a peanut butter sandwich, and one of the things a guy never considers is that peanut butter sticks to the roof of your . . . I mean, it parks itself on the top of your mouth and . . .

Help! I was drowning! I couldn't get my

tongue unglued! It had been WELDED to the top of my mouth! I'd come down with a dangerous case of Tongue Hungalosis! I smacked my lips, ran around in a tight circle, and . . .

Laughter? This was NOT funny!

It took me five minutes of steady pulling, tugging, pawing, and smacking to get my tongue back, and at that point I noticed that Doug McGrubber had stopped laughing and was looking at me with his beady little eyes. He shook his head and said, "Shep, Shep! What did I tell you? Son, I can read . . . your . . . mind."

Yeah, well, he could find something else to read, and the men could find something else to laugh about. I lifted my nose to a proud angle and went off to enjoy my own company. And I did, too. I sulked for an hour and a half and loved every minute of it.

When darkness fell, I joined Mr. Wilkens and Little Alfred inside a tent with two sleeping bags rolled out on the floor. Alfred said he wasn't tired, but two minutes after his head hit the pillow, he was gone. I curled up at the foot of his sleeping bag and watched Mr. Wilkens. By the light of a candle, he was writing in some kind of journal book.

He had been writing for, oh, ten or fifteen minutes when he looked up and saw that I was watching. "Field notes. I have to record the day's events on the site."

Oh. Swell.

"Today we exposed seven rocks on the north wall, found a peculiar rock in Slim's unit, and Doug McGrubber made the best find of the day, that bison bone in unit 3. Tomorrow, we'll map it in and take it out." For some reason, my tongue shot out of my mouth and swept across my mouth. Slurp. Mr. Wilkens gave me a peculiar look. "Did you lick your chops when I said 'bone'?"

Slurp. No, I did not.

"Bison bone."

Slurp.

"Bone."

Slurp.

He laughed. "I can't believe this. Two bones."

Slurp slurp.

"Three bones."

Slurp slurp slurp.

"Three bones with cherry pie."

Slurp slurp slurp slurp.

He doubled over with laughter. "Holy cow, you're really doing it! One more time?"

No thanks.

"Bone."

Slurp.

He wagged his head in amazement. "I've got to put this into my notes." He began writing. "'Shared my tent with a ranch dog who can count bones with his tongue.' Nobody's going to believe this!" Suddenly his laughter died and his eyes swung around to me. "Wait a second. Bison bone."

Slurp.

"Bison bone tibia digging stick."

Slurp slurp slurp.

His eyes narrowed into slits and he muttered, "Uh-oh, I think we have a problem."

Problem? Of course we had a problem. I was ready to go to sleep but he was saying ridiculous things that made me lick my chops. What kind of man does things like that?

He closed his book and laid it aside, reached into his knapsack and pulled out a roll of something gray. Duct tape. "Hank, come here."

Huh? Me? Well . . . okay. I stepped over Little Alfred's sleeping body and crept toward Mr. Wilkens. Maybe he wanted me to . . . I don't know, share his bedroll or something.

What a cheap trick! You know what he did? As soon as I got within his grabbing range, he grabbed me, threw a leg lock over my rib cage, and proceeded to . . . this was really unnecessary . . . proceeded to *wrap duct tape around both my hind legs*! I struggled against the leg irons. No luck. O treachery, I had become a captive in my own tent!

He gave me a smile—a phony counterfeit smile—and said, "There, that ought to keep you from roaming around in the night."

Roaming around? Hey, pal, did you ever hear that dogs sleep at night?

"See, as hot as it is, I'll have to leave the tent flap open." He gestured toward the tent flap. "And I'd be real disappointed if you slipped out of the tent and went looking for that . . ."

Slurp.

A grin dashed across his mouth. "I didn't say 'bone.'"

Yeah, but you cheated.

"Now, hop over there beside Alfred and let me finish my notes. Can you hop on three legs?"

Well, to be perfectly honest, I didn't know if I could "hop on three legs." How many times in a normal life does a Head of Ranch Security get mugged and shackled by his friends?

I rose to my feet and took a step . . . oops . . . I staggered sideways and fell into the middle of Little Alfred's stomach. He sat straight up and screeched, "Hankie, quit stepping on me!" He clubbed me over the head with his pillow. "Go to sleep."

Go to sleep? How could I . . . the boy rolled over before I could explain my awkward situation, and who could explain it anyway? I hopped and stumbled and staggered my way to the foot of Alfred's bedroll and collapsed, pointing myself toward the west so that I could blister my kidnapper with Eyes of Rebuke.

He was writing in his journal again, with a pair of reading glasses perched on the end of his nose. I glared nails and ice picks at him. After a while, he turned his head in my direction. "Look, I did it for your own good. Do you have any idea what Doug McGrubber would do if he caught you messing with that bison bone?"

Slurp. No, but it was a pointless question. For his information, I had lost all interest in the slurp. Bone.

"I don't know either, but he sure wouldn't be happy, after he spent all day scratching it out of the dirt. Now go to sleep and quit glaring at me."

I would glare at him as long as I wanted. I would glare at him until the sun came up, until the chickens came home to rot, until the lion laid down with the lamb, until hogs wore roller skates, until . . . moonbeam butterball waxy spinach leaves honking banana waffles . . . zzzzzzzz.

Perhaps I dozed. Yes, I'm almost sure I did,

because the next thing I knew, I had a foot in my face (Little Alfred's) and the tent was as dark as the inside of a crow. I sat up, yawned, blinked my eyes, and glanced around. And suddenly I realized that I had been dreaming about . . . bones.

Actually, that was nothing unusual. I often had bone dreams and they were always fun. Sometimes I saw myself chewing on steak bones, other times ham bones, and every once in a while, chicken bones. But this dream was different because it involved . . . well, an ancient buffalo bone. No kidding. I mean, in my dream I saw it lying in the middle of a square-shaped trench, and I was almost sure that . . .

I'd better not say any more because it might sound strange. I mean, bones don't talk, right? Yet this bone seemed to be calling out to me. Oops, I said it. Okay, in my dream, this bone was calling my name and asking . . . the bone was *pleading* for me to come and save it from "bondage."

See, I told you it would sound crazy. A talking bone! Ha ha. Boy, you never know what kind of stuff will show up in a dream.

Anyway, it was almost dawn and I had every intention of going back to sleep if Alfred would keep his feet out of my face. I dug around on the sleeping bag until I had it fluffed up just right. I flopped down, curled up in a tight circle, closed my eyes, and drifted out on a shimmering sea of . . .

"Hank! Hank the Cowdog!"

I sat straight up and lefted my lift ear . . . lefted my left ear . . . lifted my left ear, shall we say, because . . . well, I was almost sure that someone had called my name. Did you hear it? Maybe not, since you weren't there, but I did . . . or thought I did.

I switched on Earatory Scanners and did a sweep of the whole area. Nothing, not a sound . . . well, I did pick up some strange noises coming from outside the tent. I perked my ears and listened. Slim. Snoring.

False alarm. I snuggled back into my bed and rolled down my eyelids.

"Hank! Hank the Cowdog! Save me, please! They're going to lock me up in a museum!"

My head shot up. Okay, what was going on around here? I cut my eyes from side to side. Somewhere out in the darkness of night, a bone, an ancient bone, was calling me. Would I answer the call?

Hang on. It's fixing to get pretty exciting around here.

CHAPTER TWENTY

I Break Out
of Prison

Most of your ordinary mutts would have rolled over and gone back to sleep, but, fellers, ordinary has never been part of my job description.

Before I knew it, I had risen to a standing position. Someone needed to check this out. I took a step and . . .

PLOP!

You forgot that my back legs were taped together, didn't you? Me, too, and I landed on top of Little Alfred. I froze and waited to see what would happen next. The boy grumbled in his sleep and pushed me away, but he didn't wake up or club me with his pillow.

So far, so good. I lifted both ears and swung

them around to the west. There, I picked up the sounds of heavy breathing and . . . the call of a moose? Did we have meese here in the Texas Panhandle? No, wait, it was Slim snoring again. Say, that feller could really shake the rafters.

Well, if everyone was sound asleep . . . hmmm. Could I slip out of the tent without waking anyone and starting a riot? It was a Moment of Truth.

You know, very few dogs would have attempted such a bold escape. I mean, the odds against it were huge. Why, even an acrobat or a ballet dancer would have found it difficult to slip over and around two sleeping bodies—in a small tent, mind you, in the dark of night, and with his back legs tied together. But I had a feeling that I could do it.

See, years ago I had met a three-legged dog. They called him Tripod because he'd lost a leg in an accident. As I recall, he tried to run over a truck, and it didn't work out too well. But you know what? Old Tripod could get around on three legs about as well as any dog with four, and he even returned to his life's work, barking at cars.

In the back of my mind, I saw a vision of Tripod bouncing out into the street to do battle with a Volkswagen. Boink, boink, boink. That's how he did it, putting most of his weight on his front legs and hopping along on the back one.

Suddenly I felt a rush of courage. Old Tripod was an inspiration, not only to me, but to dogs all over the world. Cut off one of our legs, and we'll come back with three. Put us in shackles and chains, and we'll learn to hop. We'll never surrender, we'll never give up, because the heart of a dog is bigger than one leg!

Could I do this? YES! I would do it to honor the memory of Tripod and all the other three-legged dogs in the world who had struggled to overcome anniversary . . . university . . . who had struggled to overcome veracity . . . phooey.

It really burns me up when I'm in the middle of an inspirational speech and can't think of the right word, so let's mush on with the story.

Adversity. There we go. Dogs who had overcome adversity.

I pressed my lips together in a tight line and pointed myself toward the open tent flap.

Boink.

Boink.

Boink boink boink boink. Hey, I did it! I was standing outside the prison walls, looking up at the star full of skies and breathing the sweet air of freedom! The air had never smelled so delicious and I filled my lungs with a big gulp of it and yelled . . .

You know, this wasn't the time to be yelling, not with ten head of crabby archeologists lurking in tents, but I did think about yelling, "This one is for you, Tripod!"

And then it was time to get on with the business. I did a Broad Visual Sweep of the entire encampment to reorient myself and to make double sure that I didn't stumble into one of the men. It seemed unlikely that anyone would be wandering around camp before daylight, but a guy in my position couldn't afford to take any chances.

What was "my position"? Great question. I'm glad you asked because this business of the buffalo bone had grown into a huge struggle of wills and purposes. On the one hand, we had a crew of men who were digging up bones in the name of Science. What did they do with their bones? They put 'em in plastic bags and shipped 'em off to some museum where they would sit around in cardboard boxes forever and ever.

On the other side, we had an earnest, sincere, hardworking ranch dog who earnestly and sincerely worked hard every day and, well, had a special fondness for bones. And in case you're not familiar with the care and treatment of bones, let me point out that the very best and kindest thing you can do with a bone is . . . well, eat it.

I mean, that's why bones were put on this Earth. That's what every bone wants, to be chewed and eaten by an honest dog. No kidding.

And it just happens that the very best bones in the world are the ones that have been *aged*. Maybe you've seen dogs digging holes and burying bones? Well, there's a reason for that. We don't do it because we're bored. We do it because, while fresh bones are good, aged bones are good-times-two. Aged bones are wonderful. We're talking about flavor and tenderness. Put some age on a bone, fellers, and it becomes the kind of object that a dog thinks about in his wildest dreams.

And don't forget that I'd just had a wildest dream about bones. That's an important piece of evidence.

Do you see where this is heading? We're talking about a bone that had been aged for *seven hundred years*—not seven hundred minutes or days, but seven hundred years! I had smacked my lips over a few bones that had been aged for a week or ten days, but I couldn't even imagine the kind of deep, rich flavor you'd find in a bone that had been in the ground for seven hundred years.

So there we are. This bone deal had grown into something big and all at once we had all the ingredients of a classic You-Want-It-but-I-Want-It-More Struggle. On one side, we had Science. On the other, we had ... well, ME.

And suddenly we find ourselves at the Bottom Line: I was awake and on the prowl, heh heh, while the Agents of Science were in their respective tents, sleeping like logs and snoring like hogs.

You be the judge here, and be honest. Which side should receive the Ancient Bone Award, the dog or the Agents of Science? Come to think of it, don't bother to give your opinion because I really don't care. See, I had already made up my mind. I was going to give the coveted Ancient Bone Award to the most deserving dog I had ever known.

ME.

Yes, I was aware that I might lose a few friends in the process. I had already noticed that archeologists were pretty narrow-minded and I had every reason to suppose that they would be sore losers, especially Doug McGrubber, the same guy who had claimed that he could read my mind.

Heh heh.

Maybe he'd read the first page of my mind and maybe he'd been right about the peanut butter, but he had no idea what was fixing to happen in the next chapter. Heh heh.

He would be upset. No, he would be worse than upset. He would be badly hacked and bent out of shape. He would scream, throw his trowel, foam at the mouth, and call me hateful names . . . only I wouldn't be there to hear any of it. Heh heh. I would be long gone, like a puff of smoke in a roaring wind—me and my Ancient Bone Award.

But that brought up a small problem. Could I make my escape in leg irons? Actually, I hadn't thought that far ahead and maybe I should have. Gulp. It was quite a distance back to the ranch, and coyotes might be lurking behind every bush, but somehow I would find a way. If old Tripod could do it, so could I.

Pretty shrewd plan, huh? You bet, but don't forget who did the planning. I didn't get to be Head of Ranch Security just because of my good looks . . . which brought to mind a certain lady dog who had once enflamed my heart.

Sardina Bandana. I felt a ripple of sadness

but it was just as well that we ended it like this, without a last tearful good-bye. We had enjoyed a few fragrant moments together and we would always have those memories. She would weep for me, but that couldn't be helped.

I turned my thoughts back to the mission that lay before me, the bone rescue of the century. Was I ready? I did one last scan of all the many gauges on the console of my mind and began creeping through the darkness.

I'd better not tell you what happened next. It might scare you out of your wits.

You think you can handle this? Okay, grab hold of something solid.

I began creeping through the darkness before dawn. Boink. Boink. I began *hopping* through the so-forth, and it wasn't as easy as you might suppose. Remember all those string lines? I found two of them, but I'm no quitter. I was on a mission and nothing could stop me now.

Following the GPS reading on the illuminated screen of my mind, I inched closer and closer to the trench that held the Most Ancient of Bones.

Three feet.

Two feet.

One feet.

HUH?

You know, when a guy is out for a stroll in the moonlight, the last thing he expects to find . . . you won't believe this. I mean, it scared the living bejeebers out of me, sent a jolt of electricity down my spine, throughout my body, and almost burned off the end of my tail.

When I turned my gaze toward the Most Ancient of Bones, I saw . . .

Yipes!

My ears flew up and my eyes popped wide open. I didn't see the bone. I saw two big scruffy cannibals standing over it, staring at it with glittering eyes and licking their chops. THEY WERE ABOUT TO STEAL MY BONE!

CHAPTER TWENTY-ONE

The Cannibals Try to Steal My Bone

We had cannibals in camp and that was bad news. The badder news was that they saw me. I mean, I'd hardly made a sound yet their ears had picked it up, and their yellow eyes came up and locked on me like laser beans.

It was Rip and Snort, the two guys you never want to meet on a moonlight stroll, especially if you've recently played a nasty trick on them and mouthed off about it. Suddenly a flood of memories washed over my mind. I heard a mocking voice say, "So long, suckers!" That was my voice, in case you've forgotten. Bad idea. Very bad idea.

Gulp.

Well, what's a dog to do? In my first encounter

with them that afternoon, I had tried the path of reason and friendship. This time, I had every reason to suppose that reason and friendship wouldn't interest them much (it hadn't the first time either), so I flipped a switch that brought up the Urgent Measures program. Near panic, I skimmed through the list of U.M.s until I came to one called Back to the Tent.

Yes, Back to the Tent would work: go streaking back to the tent, dive inside, burrow under the nearest sleeping bag, and hope that the brothers wouldn't follow. Don't forget that coyotes avoid all contact with humans, so they wouldn't dare chase me into the tent.

In a flash, I turned my aircraft into the wind, closed the overhead canopy, took a deep seat, and pushed the control lever as far as it would go, up to Turbo Seven. Glancing over my shoulder at the cannibals, I shot them a grin as the rocket engines let out a scream of fire and . . .

Boink. Plop.

Okay, we had a problem. Remember the duct tape? It's impossible to launch a dog when his landing gear has been tampered with. What happens is that you get a tremendous burst of power and zero acceleration, causing the dog to, uh, crash nose-first into the ground.

That was a bad place to be, sprawled across the hard ground with my nose in the dirt, and before I could pull myself out of the wreckage, I was surrounded on all sides by grinning cannibals.

Snort seemed beside himself with glee. "Aha! Rip and Snort find dummy ranch dog away from house and boom-boom. Berry foolish you get caught by coyote brothers who feel madder and maddest about root beer trick."

After some pulling and tugging, I managed to pull my nose out of the ground. Did it hurt? You bet it hurt, but at that moment, my nose was the leets of my waries. I sat up and studied the faces of my captors. A guy never wants to make too many judgments based on first impressions, but if he did, he would say that my chances of survival looked pretty bad.

These coyotes didn't look friendly at all. We're talking about angry and stirred up—and enjoying it, too.

I tried to hide the quiver in my voice. "Listen, guys, about that root beer deal. Did I mention that sometimes you don't find it until you get down, oh, ten or fifteen feet? It's true. See, root beer is heavier than water and it sinks, so drilling for root beer is always risky. That's why we call

it 'wildcatting.' Maybe you didn't know that."

Snort curled his lip. "Coyote eat wildcat in two bites, ho ho."

"Right, but eating cats has nothing to do with drilling a wildcat root-beer well."

"Rip and Snort not want to hear big hooey about root beer. Brothers still not believe in root beer."

"Okay, let's talk about cats. You believe in cats, don't you?" No response. "Of course you do. As it happens, I've got one to sell, and I'll make you a very special deal."

They gave me blank stares. "What kind of berry spetchell deal?"

I rose to my feet, leaned toward them, and whispered, "Free, no sales tax, no commission. All you have to do is hike over to the ranch and pick up the cat, range delivery."

Snort shook his head. "Brothers not give a hoot for hike around all night."

"Okay, tell you what. I'll fetch him myself. That'll sweeten the pot even more."

"Hunk fetch cat in pot?"

"No, no, I'll fetch him from the iris patch. That's where he stays."

"Hunk catch cat in Irish pot?"

"Not Irish pot. *Iris patch*. I'll fetch the catch who stays in the Irish potch."

The brothers went into a whispering session, then Snort turned his scowling eyes back on me. "Brothers not understand about Irish fat cat."

"Okay, listen carefully. He's fat but not Irish. He stays in the iris patch and I can fetch him."

"What about Irish pot?"

"There never was an Irish pot, but if you want a cat in an Irish pot, we'll throw that into the deal. But you have to let me, uh, go back to the ranch to fetch him. What do you say?"

They stared at me for a whole minute without speaking or showing any expression. Then Snort raised his paw and clubbed me over the head. BAM! "Hunk not go nowhere and brothers not give a hoot for potted Irish cat, so Hunk shut trap."

"Fine. I was just trying to help." Well, that idea had flopped. I cut my eyes from side to side. "Okay, let's try a different approach. Bones. How do you feel about bones?"

Their tongues shot out of their mouths and their eyes lit up. "Ha! Brothers got big yum yum for bones!"

"Just what I figured. See, I noticed that you were looking at my bone in the trench."

"Trenchant bone smell berry yum yum."

"Right, and do you know why? It's ancient."

Snort shook his head. "Uh-uh. Bone trenchant, not ancient."

I took a moment to collect my thoughts. Communicating with cannibals can be difficult. "Okay, the bone is trenchant but also ancient. Do you know what that means?" Blank stares. "Ancient means old, very old."

"Trenchant bone got mold?"

"Not mold. It's *old*, even older than your grandma."

"Coyote grandma not got mold."

"I didn't say she did."

"Hunk not tell lies about coyote grandma got mold." He raised his fist.

"Wait! Let's don't do that again. My head still hurts from the last one."

He lowered his fist. "Hunk sorry for tell lies about moldy grandma?"

"Yes, yes, I'm very sorry. I don't know what came over me. Your grandma is probably the sweetest cannibal in all of Texas, so why don't you give her a bone for Christmas?"

"Too hot for Christmas."

"Okay, for her birthday . . . anniversary . . . Valentine's Day, whatever. The point is, you can give her the bone. What a gift idea, huh?"

They went into a whisper session, then Snort said, "Rip and Snort like bone more than Grandma. Not give to Grandma."

"Exactly my point. Hey, you'd be crazy to give away a bone like this and, well, you guys aren't crazy, right?"

They traded glances and laughed. "Guys pretty crazy."

"That's what I mean. You guys are crazy as bedbugs and you deserve the bone."

Snort showed me his fangs. "Guys not crazy as bunk beds."

"Okay, sorry. Forget bug banks and let's talk deal. I'm ready to give you the bone—no charge, no tax, no nothing—but I have to clear it with the, uh, sales manager." They stared at me. "It's not actually my bone, see, and the guys upstairs . . . well, they always want the last word. Ha ha. You know how they are. It's just a formality, honest."

I held my breath and waited for their reply. I mean, this was about the looniest conversation I'd ever had with anyone, but it seemed to be moving in the right direction.

Snort rolled his eyes upward. "Snort not see upstairs."

"Right. Upstairs is just an expression, a finger

of speech. Actually, the sales manager stays in that tent over there, so you give the okay and I'll just, you know, pop over to the tent and that'll be it. Ha ha."

Two pairs of empty yellow eyes stared at me. Then Snort growled, "Ha ha brothers not fall for stupid trick again."

"Yes, but let me hasten to point out . . ."

"Snort got better deal of all, break Hunk's face and take trenchant bone, too."

"Now Snort, we needn't . . ."

He leaned toward me and licked his toothy mouth. "Eat bone first, then eat Hunk, ho ho."

They were on their feet now, creeping toward me with wild hungry looks in their eyes. My mind was racing. I had to come up with something, and real fast.

The Cannibals
Eat Me

All at once I remembered something very important. Coyotes always avoid people, yet here they were in the middle of camp. Why? *Because they were burning up with thirst and had come looking for water!*

"Wait, stop! There's one last thing we need to discuss." I took a gulp of air and tried to keep my knees from knocking together. "If you guys didn't find the root beer deposits, that means you haven't had a drink all day, right? What about your boom boom thirsty?"

They didn't answer but I could see it in their eyes. I was right! I had hit the nail right on the donkey.

I plunged on. "Guys, I'll give you my bone, but

I must tell you that it's old and crumbly. If you tried to eat it with a dry mouth, you'd be disappointed, no kidding. I mean, let's go back to our example of the dry cornbread."

"Hunk not talk about corny crumblebread."

"Snort, I'm telling you this for your own good." I turned to his brother who . . . have we ever mentioned that Rip's eyes always seemed to be about half-crossed? They were. "Rip, this will be the best bone of your life. Do you want to eat it with a dry mouth?"

Rip licked his dry lips and shook his head. "Uh-uh."

"Well, there you are. It happens that we have a pan of fresh water here in camp, but it's not mine to give away. I'd have to talk to my boss . . . I mean, if you want a drink."

Snort lumbered up into my face. "Snort got plenty boss." He showed me two rows of bear-trap teeth.

"Yikes, good point."

"Hunk find water pretty quick, and not talk hooey about root beer."

I tried to hide my excitement. Hey, this plan seemed to be working! With a coyote escort on each side (they weren't taking any chances), I made my way over to the spot where Slim had left his Handy-Dandy Cowboy Wasp Trap.

"Okay, fellas, there it is. Help yourself, but I have one request. Please don't drink it all. I'm kind of thirsty myself."

The brothers roared with laughter, as if to say . . . well, as if to say that where I was going, I wouldn't need a drink. They shoved me out of the way and started lapping. I held my breath and watched.

Uh-oh. After about ten laps, Snort raised his head and spit something out of his mouth.

"Uh. Water got full of whops."

"Wasps? Oh, well, maybe you'd better not drink it."

Snort gave me a sour look and started beating his chest. "Snort not even little bit scared of whops, eat whops like candy, oh boy!"

"Well, whatever you think."

They went back to lapping. Then, uh-oh, Snort raised his head again and curled his lip. "Uh. Water got funny taste."

Oops, he'd tasted the soap. I had to act fast. "Oh, I forgot to mention that it's a little bit muddy. You probably won't like it, so . . ."

"Hunk shut trap. Rip and Snort not scared of mud. Drink muddy water like root beer, ho ho."

They stuck their heads back into the pan and

started lapping again. I watched and waited. How long would it take the soap to do its work? I had a feeling that we would see some pretty dramatic results, and it wouldn't take long.

I was right. The brothers drank so much and so fast, their bellies were dragging on the ground. They licked the bottom of the pan and ate all the dead wasps. Then they raised their heads and unleashed loud grunts of cannibal satisfaction. "Now brothers eat trenchant bone, oh boy!"

They pushed me into the trench where they could keep an eye on me, licked their respective chops, and gazed down at the Most Ancient of Bones. But then . . .

The grin on Snort's face began to fade. His eyes glazed over. He laid a paw upon his stomach. "Uh. Muddy water not feel so good in tummy-belly. Muddy water feel kind of . . ." His eyes popped wide open and he hiccuped.

HICK!

And suddenly the air was filled with thirty-seven of the prettiest soap bubbles you ever saw. On the other side of the trench, Rip did the same.

HICK!!

All at once the fearsome cannibal brothers didn't look so fearsome anymore. Their legs had turned to rubber and they were staggering

around in circles, hicking bubbles. The time had come for me to move into Phase Two.

I reached for the microphone of my mind and switched over to the Alert and Alarm Frequency. Barking in my very loudest tone of vone, I sent out the alarm:

"Attention all campers! We have coyotes inside the wire! Repeat, Charlie is inside the wire! Doug McGrubber, please report to the front! We have cannibals trying to eat your bone!"

Maybe Doug McGrubber was a light sleeper or maybe he actually did read my mind. Either way, he came flying out of his tent, carrying his pants in one hand and a flashlight in the other. He yelled, "Dog, if you mess up my bone . . ." When he saw the coyotes, he slid to a stop. The brothers stared at him with soggy eyes as foam dripped off their lips. "Jumping jiminy! Coyotes, and they've got rabies! Where's my gun?"

He made a dash for his pickup. By then I could hear the rumble of voices as the other men stuck their heads out of their tents. Rip and Snort were still stumbling in circles, staring in wonder at all the bubbles in the air.

I dived back into the trench. "Guys, I don't mean to intrude, but you need to get out of here real fast. That man went for his shotgun." No response. They didn't even look at me. "Snort, the man went for his boom-boom! Do you hear me? BOOM-BOOM!"

Snort's eyes came into focus. "Uh. Boom-boom not so healthy for coyote."

"Right, so get out of here, run for your lives! And don't stop to smell the bubbles!"

They crawled out of the trench and staggered sideways toward a line of brush about fifty yards away. It was one of the funniest sights I'd ever seen, these two ferocious cannibals running away like a couple of dizzy spiders, but there was no time to laugh and enjoy it.

By then, the other men had pulled on their jeans and had come running out of their tents, so I, uh, figured it was time to put on a little show. I took a firm three-legged grip on the ground and began firing off round after round of Heavy Duty Barks.

"And the next time you bums try to tamper with the work of science, you won't get off so lucky! The very idea, trying to eat a priceless artifact! You guys make me sick! You ought to be ashamed of yourselves, and if you're not, come back here and I'll give you a few lessons in charm and manners. I dare you! I double-dog dare you!"

It was a pretty impressive show of force and righteous anger, and as you might expect, the cowards wanted no more of me. No sir. They hit the brush and disappeared.

Mr. Wilkens and Little Alfred were the first to reach me. Wilkie raked the hair out of his eyes and gazed off in the distance. "What on Earth is going on around here?" He looked into the trench and saw the bone, then turned a stern pair of eyes on me. "Hank, were you . . . ?"

Little Alfred placed a hand on my shoulder and gave me a look of deepest concern. "Hankie, you weren't trying to eat the bone . . . were you?"

Me? Eat the bone? Why, I hardly knew what to say.

At that moment, Doug McGrubber came running up, stuffing shells into his double barrel shotgun. He snapped it shut and gazed off into the distance. "Did they get away?"

Wilkie seemed confused. "Who? What was going on out here?"

I held my breath and went to Slow Wags on the tail section. This was a crucial moment. My whole career hung in the balance.

McGrubber narrowed his eyes and chewed his lip. "When I got here, I saw two coyotes standing in my unit. And Hank here was barking." McGrubber's beady little eyes drifted down to me and all at once I felt very uncomfortable. He said,

"I'm having trouble believing this, but maybe the dog was trying to protect my bone."

Whew! My whole body went limp.

Alfred threw his arms around my neck and gave me a hug. "Hankie, I knew you were a good dog!"

Well, sure. Was there ever any doubt? The Head of Camp Security does not, repeat, does not ever eat or tamper with evidence, samples, specimens, or anything else that would contribute to the March of Science. I mean, that would be totally out of character, right?

At that moment, Slim Chance came hobbling into the crowd, bent over and walking like a crab. "What's all the noise?"

Mr. Wilkens explained that I had, well, made a hero of myself and saved The Most Ancient of Bones. Slim uttered a grunt (don't forget, he speaks Gruntlish in the mornings) and went back to his bed, again limping like an old man.

Wilkie noticed. "What's wrong with you?"

Slim muttered, "I feel like I was dropped out of an airplane."

"Next time you go camping, bring an air mattress, like the rest of us."

Slim kept walking. "It ain't manly."

Wilkie laughed and shook his head. "He's really stubborn, isn't he?"

Yes, exactly! I'd been saying that for years, and nobody had ever listened to me.

Well, it was almost daylight, so Wilkie built a fire and boiled a big pot of coffee, while some of the other men started cooking breakfast. Just as Wilkie was passing out tin cups of steaming coffee to the crew, we heard the sound of an approaching vehicle. We all turned and saw . . .

That was odd. It appeared to be a pickup . . . Loper's pickup, in fact. He drove up to the site and got out.

Wilkens handed him a cup and Alfred walked over to him. "Hi, Dad. What are you doing here?"

Loper took a sip of coffee and laid a hand on the boy's shoulder. "I didn't sleep well last night. I'm ashamed of myself for not coming over here with you yesterday."

The boy seemed surprised. "Well, you had to haul water, I guess."

"Slim could have hauled the water. The cows aren't fussy."

"Yeah, but you don't like arkimology. You said so."

Loper looked into Alfred's face and smiled.

"But I like *you*, son, and I'm your dad. A daddy ought to be with his boy before he's grown and gone. I was just thinking of myself and I'm sorry." Loper turned to Mr. Wilkens. "As far as I know, I've got no talent for this stuff, but I'm willing to learn, if you'll put up with me."

Alfred hugged his dad. "I'm glad you came. It'll be fun."

Slim Chance came limping up just then. "Yeah, you'll love it, Loper . . . but tomorrow you won't be able to walk. This stuff ain't for sissies."

That drew a big laugh, then the men formed a line and loaded their plates with scrambled eggs and bacon. I was astonished when Stork Legs Witt, the same flint-heart who had refused to share his ham sandwich the night before, gave me a plate of my very own. Wow! It was one of the proudest moments of my career.

And that's about all the story. No, wait. There's more, and it's pretty interesting.

The Amazing
Conclusion

Here's the rest of the story. After breakfast, the men stacked their dishes in a washtub and went to their units to begin the day's work. As Wilkie was leaving the breakfast area, Stork Legs Witt caught him by the arm.

"Hey, boss, you know that rock in Slim's unit? I did some research last night and it's not a rock." He flipped open a big book and pointed to a photograph. "Look at this."

Wilkie glanced at the picture, then looked closer and smacked his hand against his forehead. "A mammoth tooth? That's impossible! How can you have a twelve-thousand-year-old mammoth tooth in a house that dates to 1300 A.D.?"

Witt pointed to Little Alfred, who was standing

nearby. "My guess is that one day, seven hundred years ago, a little feller like him was out on a hike and dug it out of the creek bank. He did what little boys have always done—brought it home and gave it to his mom, and she kept it in a special place."

Wilkie chuckled to himself. "I guess that makes sense, and it kind of brings the past to life, doesn't it?" He turned to Alfred. "Well, kiddo, it's not exactly a dinosaur, but it's close enough. You got your wish, and it's going to make a great addition to my report."

Pretty neat, huh? Alfred was thrilled and that's about the end of the . . . wait. One last thing.

When the crew went back to work, I found myself . . . well, a bit restless. Bored, shall we say. After scratching a couple of fleas, I happened to glance around and saw . . .

Guess who was sitting in the back of her pickup, gazing at me with adoring brown eyes. Heh heh. After checking to be sure her ugly brother wasn't lurking around, I drifted over to the pickup and gave her a wolfish smile.

"What do you think now, sweet thang?"

"Well, you came out of that smelling like a rose."

"Thank you, thank you."

"But you know what they say."

"What do they say, darlin'? I'm dying to hear."

She leaned toward me and whispered, "When you're lucky, you don't need brains."

I stiffened. "I have no idea what you mean by that, madame."

"Look, Leroy, I was awake and saw the whole thing. If those coyotes hadn't blundered into camp, you would have stolen that bone and there would be a price on your head right now."

I beamed her a look of righteous indigestion. "You know, I think it's over between us, and for your information, my name is not Leroy."

"Yeah? Well, here's a flash. My name isn't Sardina, and I don't have a sister."

"That's not possible. I met her myself."

"And I don't have a brother named Choo Choo."

"Huh? You mean . . . ?"

"Meathead."

Anyway, it was mostly a great day, and I'd never had the slightest interest in that woman from Boston. The next time she meets a lobster on the beach, I hope it bites her right on the end of her snooty little nose.

The important thing is that I had solved The Case of the Most Ancient Bone and had won the

hearts of arkinsawlogists all over Texas. The excavation went on for three more days and the guys from our ranch stayed for the whole thing. They even decided that it was pretty interesting work . . . although I must report that after one night of camping The Cowboy Way, Slim slipped away for an hour and came back with an air mattress. I have no idea where he found it.

Oh, and I'm proud to report that when I got back to the ranch, I caught Mister Kitty Precious outside the yard and away from his iris patch. Tee hee. I ran him up a tree and barked at him for three solid hours, until Sally May . . .

Never mind. The point is that I enjoyed another huge moral victory over the cat and lived everly happy afterly, and this story is finished.

Case closed.

The following activities are samples from *The Hank Times*, the official newspaper of Hank's Security Force. Do not write on these pages unless this is your book. Even then, why not just find a scrap of paper?

Cowboy Decoder

Cowboy Decoding Information

	1	2	3	4	5	6
A	E	O	S	O	C	A
B	V	N	P	W	L	G
C	B	K	T	I	U	H

Use the cowboy decoder (above) to unscramble the following message from a mystery person that was overheard on the ranch. It was intercepted by none other than Hank.

B4 A6 C2 A1   C5 B3   B3 A4 A2 A5 C6

" _ _ _ _ _ _ _ _ _ _ _ _,

B4 A1 B1 A1   B6 A4 C3   C3 C6 C4 B2 B6 A3

    _ _ _ _ _ _ _ _ _ _ _ _ _

C3 A2   C3 A6 B5 C2   A6 C1 A2 C5 C3

_ _ _ _ _ _ _ _ _ _ _."

Answer:

"Photogenic" Memory Quiz

We all know that Hank has a "photogenic" memory—being aware of your surroundings is an important quality for a Head of Ranch Security. Now you can test your powers of observation.

How good is your memory? Look at the illustration on page 56 and try to remember as many things about it as possible. Then turn back to this page and see how many questions you can answer.

1. Was the man wearing a watch? Yes or No?

2. How full of lemonade was the pitcher? Full, two-thirds full, or half full?

3. Could you see the DRIVER'S seatbelt? Yes or No?

4. Was Little Alfred winking with his Left or Right eye?

5. What was the number on the pickup? 10, 70, or 100?

6. How many of Little Alfred's hands could you see? 1, 2, or 3?

A Big Case

I t's me again, Hank the Cowdog. It was almost time for supper scraps, and I was waiting and ready. They, were gone! Did my scraps end up in someone else's tummy? The Head of Ranch Security is about to find out what happened! So help me conduct an investigation. We'll go strictly by the numbers. Follow the conversation and we will solve The Case of the Missing Scraps!

1. **Pick a number from 5 to 8** ——

2. Sally May
"I fixed you a *double* portion of scrambled eggs this morning."
Let's double our number ——

3. Loper
"Good, I'll be *lucky* if I'm in at *six*."
Let's add 6 ——

4. Little Alfred
"Mommy, can I have *two more* stwips of bacon pwease?"
Let's add 2 ——

5. Sally May
"I'm expecting the choir ladies to be here *around ten* this morning."
Let's round our number to the nearest 10 ——

6. Pete
"Hey Hankie. Do you think you can figure this out with *two more* clues?"
Let's add 2 ____

7. Hank
"Ha! I think I can figure things out in *half* the time it would take you, Kitty Kitty.
Let's divide our number in half ____

8. It's time to crack open our code book and bring all these clues together and solve this case.
Let's map the letter to a number in the alphabet (1=A, 2=B, 3=C, etc...) ____

9. **Pick any state that begins with our letter above** ____

10. **Let's be on the safe side and pick another state that begins with our letter** ____

11. My scraps are in someone's tummy. **Pick an animal that begins with our letter and has a pouch.** ____

Answer:

Have you read all
of Hank's adventures?

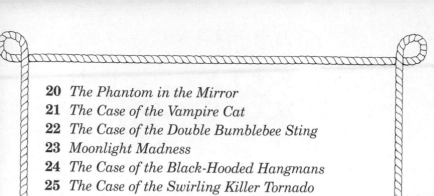

Join Hank the Cowdog's Security Force

Are you a big Hank the Cowdog fan? Then you'll want to join Hank's Security Force. Here is some of the neat stuff you will receive:

Welcome Package
- A Hank paperback of your choice
- A free Hank bookmark

Eight issues of *The Hank Times* newspaper
- Stories about Hank and his friends
- Lots of great games and puzzles
- Special previews of future books
- Fun contests

More Security Force Benefits
- Special discounts on Hank books and audiotapes
- An original Hank poster (19" x 25") absolutely free
- Unlimited access to Hank's Security Force website at www.hankthecowdog.com

Total value of the Welcome Package and *The Hank Times* is $23.95. However, your two-year membership is **only $8.95** plus $4.00 for shipping and handling.

☐ Yes, I want to join Hank's Security Force. Enclosed is $12.95 ($8.95 + $4.00 for shipping and handling) for my **two-year membership**. [Make check payable to Maverick Books. International shipping extra.]

WHICH BOOK WOULD YOU LIKE TO RECEIVE IN YOUR WELCOME PACKAGE? CHOOSE ANY BOOK IN THE SERIES.

_____

YOUR NAME   **BOY or GIRL** (CIRCLE ONE)

_____

MAILING ADDRESS

_____

CITY   STATE   ZIP

_____

TELEPHONE   BIRTH DATE

Are you a ☐ Teacher or ☐ Librarian?

E-MAIL

Send check or money order for $12.95 to:

Hank's Security Force
Maverick Books
P.O. Box 549
Perryton, Texas 79070

DO NOT SEND CASH.
OFFER SUBJECT TO CHANGE.
Allow 3–4 weeks for delivery.

The Hank the Cowdog Security Force, the Welcome Package, and The Hank Times *are the sole responsibility of Maverick Books. They are not organized, sponsored, or endorsed by Penguin Group (USA) Inc., Puffin Books, Viking Children's Books, or their subsidiaries or affiliates.*